WITHDRAWN

THE GEORGIA REGIONAL
LIBRARY FOR THE BLIND
AND PHYSICALLY
HANDICAPPED IS A FREE
SERVICE FOR INDIVIDUALS
UNABLE TO READ
STANDARD PRINT.

ASK AT OUR CIRCULATION
DESK HOW TO REGISTER
FOR THIS SERVICE, AS WELL
AS OTHER SERVICES
OFFERED BY THIS LIBRARY.

D1398576

Ralph Compton

The Abilene
Trail

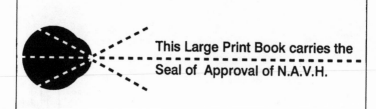

This Large Print Book carries the
Seal of Approval of N.A.V.H.

Ralph Compton

The Abilene
Trail

A Ralph Compton Novel
by Dusty Richards

NEWTON COUNTY LIBRARY SYSTEM
7116 FLOYD STREET, N.E.
COVINGTON, GA 30014

Thorndike Press • Waterville, Maine

Copyright © The Estate of Ralph Compton, 2003

Map copyright © New American Library, 2003

Trail Drive Series

All rights reserved.

This is a work of fiction. Names, characters, places, and incidents either are the product of the author's imagination or are used fictitiously, and any resemblance to actual persons, living or dead, business establishments, events, or locales is entirely coincidental.

Published in 2004 by arrangement with NAL Signet, a member of Penguin Group (USA) Inc.

Thorndike Press® Large Print Western.

The tree indicium is a trademark of Thorndike Press.

The text of this Large Print edition is unabridged.
Other aspects of the book may vary from the original edition.

Set in 16 pt. Plantin by Al Chase.

Printed in the United States on permanent paper.

Library of Congress Cataloging-in-Publication Data

Richards, Dusty.
    The Abilene Trail : a Ralph Compton novel / by Dusty Richards.
        p. cm.
    At head of title: Ralph Compton.
    ISBN 0-7862-6439-X (lg. print : hc : alk. paper)
    1. Cattle drives — Fiction.   2. Cattle stealing — Fiction.
3. Texas Cattle Trail — Fiction.   4. Texas — Fiction.
5. Large type books.   I. Compton, Ralph.   II. Title.
PS3568.I31523A64 2004
    813'.54—dc22   2004047917

I'm dedicating this book to Jim Parker of Yukon, Oklahoma, a grand man who dedicated his life to preserving the history of the Chisholm Trail; to Cotton Clem, who went with me to learn all about the cattle road; and to the National Chuckwagon Racing Championship that each Labor Day weekend on the Bar Eoff Ranch, Clinton, Arkansas, keeps our Western traditions alive and rolling.

— Dusty Richards

National Association for Visually Handicapped
------------------------- *serving the partially seeing*

As the Founder/CEO of NAVH, the only national health agency solely devoted to those who, although not totally blind, have an eye disease which could lead to serious visual impairment, I am pleased to recognize Thorndike Press* as one of the leading publishers in the large print field.

Founded in 1954 in San Francisco to prepare large print textbooks for partially seeing children, NAVH became the pioneer and standard setting agency in the preparation of large type.

Today, those publishers who meet our standards carry the prestigious "Seal of Approval" indicating high quality large print. We are delighted that Thorndike Press is one of the publishers whose titles meet these standards. We are also pleased to recognize the significant contribution Thorndike Press is making in this important and growing field.

Lorraine H. Marchi, L.H.D.
Founder/CEO
NAVH

* Thorndike Press encompasses the following imprints: Thorndike, Wheeler, Walker and Large Print Press.

THE IMMORTAL COWBOY

This is respectfully dedicated to the "American Cowboy." His was the saga sparked by the turmoil that followed the Civil War, and the passing of more than a century has by no means diminished the flame.

True, the old days and the old ways are but treasured memories, and the old trails have grown dim with the ravages of time, but the spirit of the cowboy lives on.

In my travels — to Texas, Oklahoma, Kansas, Nebraska, Colorado, Wyoming, New Mexico, and Arizona — I always find something that reminds me of the Old West. While I am walking these plains and mountains for the first time, there is this feeling that a part of me is eternal, that I have known these old trails before. I believe it is the undying spirit of the frontier calling, allowing me, through the mind's eye, to step back into time. What is the appeal of the Old West of the American frontier?

It has been epitomized by some as the dark and bloody period in American history. Its heroes — Crockett, Bowie, Hickok, Earp — have been reviled and criticized. Yet the Old West lives on, larger than life.

It has become a symbol of freedom, when there was always another mountain to climb and another river to cross; when a dispute between two men was settled not with expensive lawyers, but with fists, knives, or guns. Barbaric? Maybe. But some things never change. When the cowboy rode into the pages of American history, he left behind a legacy that lives within the hearts of us all.

— *Ralph Compton*

The Abilene Trail

Introduction

During the Civil War, the American people ate every chicken and pig in the land. After that conflict, the industrialized North was hungry for protein. In Texas and old Mexico, there were thousands of unbranded longhorn cattle for the catching.

In the years following their bitter defeat, many impoverished Texans headed large cattle herds toward that old North Star, looking for the rich markets. Some returned to brag of their success; others cursed their bad luck, for they lost fortunes in cattle to bushwhackers, rustlers, irate farmers, and natural disasters.

An Illinois farmer, Joe McCoy, spent two years trying to convince one of the railroads to set up shipping yards beyond the sod buster's Texas Tick Fever deadlines. At last, this ambitious man in his simple store-bought clothing and muddy shoes found a railroad president who took him seriously.

Joe McCoy started building loading pens at Abilene, Kansas, in the fall of 1867. That winter McCoy hired a surveyor and his sons to plow a furrow from his pens at Abilene to near the site of Jesse Chisholm's trading post (Wichita, Kansas) to show them the way. Joe also sent salesmen to Texas armed with posters showing this route west of the trouble with farmers and the promise of a good market.

The trail was known as the Abilene Trail until the early 1870s, when the drovers began calling it Jesse's Trail.

Chapter 1

November 21, 1867
Kerr Mac County, Texas

"You ever been to Kansas, Mark?" he asked the wide-eyed teenager.

"Kansas?" The youth threw his hands up to shade his eyes from the noontime sun. "Hell — I mean, no, sir."

Ben McCollough looked over at the woman who had come to the doorway of the paintless house. At thirty-two, Jenny Fulton was an attractive enough widow with three boys. Mark, her eldest, stood before Ben's roan horse, all eaten up with the notion of being asked to make his first cattle drive. The light brown-haired woman standing in the threshold could use the money her son would earn. As a consideration to her, Ben would have to see that some of the boy's pay managed to make it home.

"Hello, Jenny," he said, straightening his spine in the saddle and removing his high crown hat for her. Her willowy figure in the

13

faded, wash-worn dress was enough to make his guts roil.

"Hello, Ben. You must be needing some help today." The warm smile showed her even, white teeth, and she pushed back an errant wave of hair from her face. Her steps looked dainty as she walked toward them. By her age, most women's feet were splayed out from being without shoes so long — but not Jenny's.

"I was asking Mark if he had time to go to Kansas this next spring."

"I see," she said, using her hand to hold back her hair and also shade her eyes. "He'll turn sixteen next month."

"I know. Been some younger boys than that go up the trail. Could you spare him for a few months?"

"Sixteen these days and you're a man, aren't you?" She shook her head as if in mild disbelief.

He stepped off the roan and dropped the reins. All summer and half the fall he'd thought about courting her and done nothing. A couple of times he'd sent a deer carcass over so she and the boys had meat. His cook, Hap, had delivered them to her. Each time afterward she sent him a nice thank-you note in her gracious penmanship with a whiff of sweet perfume on the notes.

"Yes, I reckon the war . . ." He regretted mentioning the war. The conflict had taken her husband, Allen Fulton, leaving her with the three small boys to raise alone.

"Changed all our lives," she said, and nodded.

"If it's all right, then Mark needs to get his gear ready. I've got him a good saddle at the ranch." Ben knew the boy's worn-out saddle would never make it up the trail.

"Mark?" she said.

"Yes?"

"I guess you better tell Mr. McCollough what you aim to do."

"Go to Kansas!" he shouted, and threw his felt hat in the air. "Yahoo!"

"Well, how many more hands do you have hired, Ben?"

"Actually, he's the first."

"That's a nice compliment," she said to her eldest.

Ben nodded that he heard her. "Hap has a good milk cow over at the ranch. I need to board her while we're going up the trail."

Her face beamed at his offer. "I'd sure be pleased to have one. My heifer's went dry."

"Guess tomorrow, then, Mark can make his first cattle drive and get Jersey over here."

"Thanks, Ben," she said with her gaze focused on the ground. She looked up, wetting her lips. "I do appreciate the many things you've done for me and the boys."

He shook his head to dismiss her compliment.

"No." She reached out and patted his arms folded over his chest. "You need to come over and have supper with us. So we can repay your generosity."

He felt trapped. No need in her fixing him supper — why, she had trouble enough feeding her boys, let alone feeding him. Where she'd touched his forearm, he noticed the spot felt on fire. "I'll be real busy —"

"You have to eat sometime. You can send word by Mark. But promise you will come eat with us one night?"

"I will . . . I'll come eat with you."

A warm smile of relief swept her smooth face, and her blue eyes twinkled.

At thirty-nine years old, he worried about their age difference. He wasn't a kid any longer, though at times he felt like one, especially when his thoughts ran to her. Lots more things to worry about than his mushy feelings. There were a million details to getting a cattle drive on the way, and this shipping point at Abilene wasn't next door — a far ways from it.

16

He put his hat back on his head. Even in her working clothes, though he wondered if she owned any better, she looked nice. But was he ready for a woman in his life? This trail drive could be the difference between his being some two-bit rancher and being a real one. Maybe . . . maybe after the drive he would finally need a lady in his life.

"Mark, you come over tomorrow and get the jersey cow for your mom. Then ride back the next day and take you a bunk. We've got lots of getting ready to do."

"Thanks, mister — I mean, Ben."

"What night are we having this supper?" he asked her.

"Sunday night soon enough?"

"Yes, ma'am. Don't go to no bother, hear me?"

"Oh, no. Just be usual fare."

"Thanks. See you Sunday," he said, and reined the roan around for home. What had he agreed to? Only eating supper with her so far. What could that hurt? On one hand, he wanted her for his own; on the other, he wasn't damn well certain that he wanted a woman like a ship's anchor around his neck. So what would it be? He'd have to see. Have to figure it all out somehow.

At sunup, Hap was pouring coffee in

Ben's cup. The grizzle-faced former sergeant swung around the stiff leg that he had received at the battle of Pea Ridge and gathered their breakfast dishes. Both stock dogs were raising Cain out front of the house when Ben went to the kitchen window to see who was out there.

"Mark's already come for the jersey cow," he said, amazed how early the boy must have gotten up to have ridden there. He'd completely forgotten about the anxiousness of youth.

"Making her that cow as a gift?" the white-whiskered cook asked.

"Loaning it to her while we go to Kansas."

"Loaning it?" Hap scoffed. "We talked about selling her last I heard anything about her."

"Aw, shut up. I told you her cow died. It's for her use till we get back."

"I ain't milking two cows when we get back."

"Hush up 'fore that boy hears us arguing."

"By damn, Ben McCulloughie, I don't aim to milk two old cows."

"No one asked you to — now hush."

Hap went off grumbling to himself and rattling metal pans in the dry sink, doing the dishes.

18

"Come on in, Mark," Ben said to the boy, who stood with his hat in his hand in the doorway. "Better yet, you wash up out there and then come in. Hap, you have any food left for a starving boy?"

"How can he be starving?" Hap asked with his hands set upon his narrow hips.

" 'Cause all teenage boys have got a holler leg for food."

"I'll whip him up some eggs," Hap said, sounding put-out and making lots of noise taking the covers off the top to restoke the fire in the range. "A damn cook's job is never done around here."

"But ain't you lucky," Ben said, blowing the steam off his coffee.

"How's that?"

"You've got someone to cook for." Ben chuckled to himself.

"You think I can't find work? Let me tell you, Ben McCulloughie, I can find work quicker than you can blink your eyes."

"Sure you can, Hap. Why, there's lots of greasy-sack outfits going up the trail would love to have you cooking for them."

"And I ain't never going to Kansas with no damn pack train. I could find me a job with a wagon outfit."

"Why?"

"What do you mean, why?"

19

"You've already got a job with one with me."

Hap scratched his sideburns. "Now you've gone and made me forget why I was so mad at you in the first place."

Ben knew the answer, but he damn sure wasn't going to remind his cook. There'd be lots of time on the trail to think about all of it — for him the picture of Jenny Fulton standing in the doorway the day before was going to eat a hole in his guts before he ever got out of Texas.

Chapter 2

Ben spent most of the morning making more plans for the drive. Through the open front doorway, he could look across the brown grass meadows to Cooter's Bluff above Wild Hoss Creek. The horse herd he had begun to collect for the drive was grazing in the bottom: bays, blacks, a few grays, and some roans. He'd need at least five head per man. Sunlight danced on the cedars and live oaks. November was good time in the hill country. This cattle-driving business could provide him with the land to expand his herd. At thirty-nine, he couldn't expect to forever be some two-bit rancher — the MC brand needed to be on more mother cows. He needed a couple of them purebred roan bulls to use on his longhorns. Ranching wouldn't always be rounding up wild-as-deer cattle mavericks out of the brakes and mesquite thickets.

He drummed his finger on the letter that Col. Joe McCoy's man, William Blair, had left. *North is hungry for beef. Top steers will bring as much as forty dollars per head at our new pens in Abilene, Kansas.* Forty dollars. Ben tried to erase the price tag from his mind. Four-year-old steers on the Mexican border could be bought for a few dollars. Even if he could sell enough of them at, say, twenty bucks, the size ranch he wanted could be a reality at those prices.

The best interest rate he could find so far was fifty percent. For that loan he had to pledge all his resources, ranch, horses, and mother cows. But he could borrow up to three thousand dollars — that would be enough by his mathematics to purchase eight hundred head of steer and head them for Kansas when the grass broke its dormancy next spring.

He drummed his fingertips on the tabletop. If he failed he'd have nothing but his callused hands, and he'd have to start all over, like when he came back from the war. That was why he had not dared court Jenny Fulton the past year. His whole life teetered on making a successful drive — then he could make plans for a future life. He listened to the horses and then the drum of hoofbeats. Someone was coming. He rose to his full six-foot-four and stretched his hands over his head. The reach took some of the stiffness out of his back — he felt more and more of that tightness getting up in the morning.

"Mr. McCollough, you home, sir?"

He ducked the lintel and straightened to smile at the freckle-faced boy Mark's age. Billy Jim Watts was riding a long-headed bay horse.

"Mark said you was hiring hands to go to Kansas."

Ben nodded. "You come to apply."

"I sure . . . Yes, sir."

"Kin you rope?"

"Some."

"Kin you ride a pitching horse?"

"If I can't I can sure get on him again." He dismounted off his bay and jerked his wash-worn pants down so they fit more comfortable.

Amused at the eager boy's answers, Ben chuckled in his throat. "Your mama know what you're doing?"

"Yes, sir."

"How'd she take it?"

"Like most women." Billy Jim made a face. "Kinda wet-eyed. You know what I mean?"

Ben shook his head ruefully. "Listen, there ain't no wanting to go home on this deal. It'll be pure hell most of the time. No complaining, no turning back. Can you swim?"

Billy Jim squinted his green eyes, looking at Ben with a pained expression. "What for?"

" 'Cause they tell me we've got forty rivers to cross to get to Abilene."

"I can swim."

"Can you shoot?"

"I done shot a twenty-two lots."

"I was more in mind of a pistol."

The youth nodded; then he cocked his head to the side to look up at Ben. "I can damn sure learn. What I mean is, sir, I can learn real quick."

"I'll keep you in mind, Billy Jim. Tell your mom and daddy I said hi."

"Means I don't get the job?"

"I'm taking it under advisement."

"That like setting a hen on top of hatching eggs?"

Ben chuckled and so did the youth. "Check with me about Christmastime."

He watched the youth awkwardly mount the slab-sided bay, which about fell over in the process. Poor round-bottomed boy — a real miracle he could even stay in the saddle; he bounced all over it when he rode. Billy Jim said thanks and left in a trot, bobbing up and down like a cork with a pan fish on the other end of the line. Ben drew a deep breath up his nose. He needed to fill out the rest of his roster with grown men. There were enough ex-soldiers grubbing a living who could use the work. No, one teenager on the trail with him was plenty. He already had Mark.

He saddled up his roan horse and headed for Teeville. Hap and Mark were out checking the cows and calves, while in town he'd see who he could get signed up as drovers. Plus he wanted to talk to Ab Bowers about the loan. He'd need some of the money after the first of the year.

Teeville sat on the banks of Morgan Creek: two stores, bank, saddlery, doctor's office over it, gunsmith, two saloons, a one-room schoolhouse, and a Methodist church, plus a smattering of small houses around the edge. It was a quiet place with a few curs to announce who came and went. Deputy sheriff Wylie Harold kept the peace; he had a small jail that sat empty most of the time, and he reported to the sheriff over at the county seat.

Ben checked the post office in Whitaker's store. A letter had come from Colonel Mc-Coy's man Blair assuring him there would be plenty of buyers and shipping cars when he arrived with his herd in Abilene next summer. The plowed furrow to mark the way from the Arkansas River crossing to the shipping pens was progressing fine and would be completed before spring broke green on the prairie as a guide for him to follow.

Ben put the letter in his vest and thanked Mr. Whitaker.

"You still planning to make a drive next year?" the gray-headed storekeeper asked.

"Figured so."

"Well, me and the missus, we've been talking. You buy your supplies from me, I'll carry them on the books. I figure if anyone can get through that mess of Indian and crazy jayhawk farmers up there, you can, Ben." Whitaker wiped his hands on his white apron. "Ain't making that offer to many folks, Ben. You know that some won't ever come back?"

Ben nodded. "I appreciate your offer. I'll be thinking on it."

"Be New Year's 'fore you know it," Whitaker said, and shook his head. "Years get to going by faster."

"They sure do." Ben left the store and headed for the bank. Whitaker's offer sounded good. It would save him from borrowing so much money that way, even though he'd still feel as obligated to the storekeeper as he would to his banker for the loan.

Perhaps he needed to go see his cattle buyer on the border. If everyone got the idea they were heading north with a herd, it might make cattle higher to buy down there. He had the grass to winter them and calm them down — most drovers would wait until almost spring, buy them, then drive them up the road. His plan was to settle them, as well as put some weight on his herd. If he could weed out the real spooky troublemakers, perhaps the drive would go smoother.

At the bank he spoke to Ab Bowers. The bald man with the bushy white sideburns acted pleased he'd dropped in. They sat at his polished walnut desk and visited, with sunlight streaming in the window.

"How's things going, Ben?"

"Like I've planned. I'm going to see Martinez and talk about what he can buy down there."

"Good plan you've got." Bowers tented his hands in front of his nose, palm-to-palm, and nodded in approval. "You're the only one I know with a real design to this drive business. Getting those cattle up here and sorting out the wild ones . . . Yes, sir — good thinking. Most drovers come in here scoff at the notion. Want to gather them and head out, trail-break them on the way."

"Wild cattle lose weight," Ben said.

"Exactly!" The banker pointed his clasped hands at him. "Exactly."

"I may need that money in the next few weeks."

"It'll be ready, Ben, any day you need it."

He left the bank satisfied that part of his business was in place and went across the street for a beer and the free counter lunch in the Cattleman's Saloon. Earnie nodded from behind the bar and held up a schooner for him to approve.

"I'll take one," Ben said, looking around as he took a place at the bar.

"Been staying busy, Ben?" the short, swarthy-faced man asked, working the tap and filling the glass.

"Busy enough. Ernie, you let out the word I need about four good cowhands next spring."

"Going north," the man said with a whimsical shake of his head.

"Taking a herd up."

"I'll do that. Shouldn't be any problem getting hands. Not much paying work around here," Ernie said.

"I need men that will work."

"I know. I won't send you no lazy ones."

"Well, if it ain't Captain Ben Mac, hisself," someone said behind his back.

He turned mildly at the woman's voice. Millescent Burns stood a few feet away, her steel-blue eyes taking him in. She wore a dress of layered lace, low-cut so that most of her bare, flat chest bones were exposed between her breasts. In her twenties, she let her hair hang loose in long, dishwater-blond curls that looked a little matted to him. The knife scar down her right cheek she kept hidden most of the time with her hair. Teeville's leading shady lady appraised him.

"How've you been, Milly?" he asked, considering the beer.

"Not worth a damn. You ain't been to see me."

He looked at her hard. "I've not been to see you in over a year, Milly."

"Well, so what?" She threw a strip of lace over her shoulder as if to free herself of it. "Looks to me like we need to change that. You ain't no stick-in-the-mud churchgoer now, are you, Captain?"

He turned back, rested his elbows on the bar, and watched her in the mirror. Slow-like, he took another swallow of the cool beer. She moved in and joined him with her back to the bar and twirling the strip of lace, close enough that her familiar perfume and musk soon filled his nose.

"You afraid you might like me again?" she asked softly.

"I'm afraid of lots of things."

"Oh, no, Captain, I seen you throw that drunk out the door one night who was slapping me. I mean, he took bird-flying lessons from that toss."

"I didn't hold with him slapping a woman."

She twisted around, raising her arms up to put them on the bar. Less than five feet tall, the dove had trouble reaching the counter with her elbows. "I could sure pay you back for doing that, Captain."

He shook his head, finished the beer, and put down a dime to pay for it. With a tip of his hat to her, he headed for the bat-wing doors.

"You know a woman scorned can be dangerous, Captain."

He paused before pushing outside. "You have a nice day, Milly."

"Go to hell!" she shouted after him. "I can have any man I want. And I gawdamn sure don't want you."

Her words stung him. He stood in the shade of the saloon's false front on the boardwalk. Whatever they'd had together was over — he'd learn to not go back in there for another horsewhipping. Millescent did what she wanted, and no one man was ever enough for her.

He checked the cinch and swung up on the roan. He'd better get home — he wanted to be on his way to the border before daylight. One more picture of the defiant Milly swinging the strip of lace over her shoulder made his guts churn — it was all over. She could have any man she wanted, and she would before the day was over. He set the roan to a long trot and left Teeville.

"Supper's ready, if you two varmints aim to eat tonight," Hap announced from the kitchen doorway.

"We better get in there," Mark said, on his feet. "I'd hate to miss it."

"Me too," Ben said, getting up from the stuffed chair.

"You boys have a good day?" Ben asked, ducking through the doorway and straightening to look at the food spread on the table.

"Call it good, if you like," Hap grumbled. "We rode our butts off and finally found most of the cowherd up in the canyons."

"You've got six new calves," Mark said.

"That helps," Ben said in approval. "Oh, Hap, Mark and I are going to the border in the morning. I want to be certain Martinez is going to have those steers."

Hap looked at the two of them and shook his head. "You boys better be careful down there."

Ben shared a private wink with Mark. "We will be."

Seated at the table, and fixing their plates, they listened to Hap gripe about having to get up so early and fix them breakfast, with them leaving at that time.

"Bet that beats going up the trail with a greasy-sack outfit," Ben said, and passed the plate of biscuits on to Mark.

"Greasy-sack outfit! I ain't going up no trail with one of them!" Hap blustered about that for several minutes.

"What's that mean — greasy sack?" Mark asked.

"Means an outfit's too cheap to have a wagon," Hap explained. "Means they got all their cooking gear and grub in tow sacks slung over a horse. Now, wouldn't a cook fix real good meals for working hands? Land's sake, that would be worse than eating mud pies."

"Guess we'll have to take a wagon, Mark, or cook for ourselves." Ben laughed.

Amused, Mark nodded.

"Cook for yourselves, huh? You two ain't a threat to no one about cooking. The dang flies would have a pie supper to raise money to screen out your kitchen. And another thing: I ain't driving no damn dumb oxen to Kansas either. So you'd better start looking for mules or a new cook."

"Mules?" Ben frowned at him.

"Mules!" Hap pointed his fork at him.

Ben noticed that Mark kept his head down to conceal his amusement.

Before daybreak, the two rode south. Ben had given Mark a small .30-caliber Colt and holster to wear on the trip. The gun belt fit the youth, and he nodded in approval after he strapped it on.

"It's loaded." Ben said. "Don't never draw it unless you need it. When you need it, then use it. Sometime it will be the difference between you living or whoever wants to kill you doing the same."

Mark nodded that he understood, and they went for the horses.

Ben decided an older man like himself couldn't tell everything about life to someone like Mark; some things the boy had to learn on the way. The notion went over and over in Ben's mind, because the next day they'd arrive in a land where life was cheap and not much emotion was shed over the dead, save how their few valuables would be divided by those living when the gunsmoke cleared.

In Harper, they ate supper in a café after sundown. The dark-eyed girl who waited on them took a shine to Mark. She even brought him some extra sopapillas and thick, dark honey in a small white bowl. He acted more pleased with the treat than the tail-swishing young woman who served it. The whole matter amused Ben.

"I'd sleep in a bed here tonight, but they usually have bedbugs that bite," Ben said. "Let's ride out of town and sleep under the stars tonight."

"Fine with me."

They left the café and stood on the board-walk in the night. Ben thought about going into a bar for a beer, then reconsidered as they rode out of town. Along a creek they found a place to hobble their horses and spread out their bedding.

"Ben, I guess this is as far as I've ever been away from home," Mark said from his bedroll beside him.

"Bet it is," Ben agreed, thinking about the war and his nights away from home in the cold and the rain. This would be a good one by that comparison.

They crossed the Rio Bravo into Aqua Fría beneath the noon sun. Coming out of the knee-deep water, their animals clambered with wet hooves over the smooth rocks onto the Mexican side. Adobe hovels covered the hillside, and several topless women, young and old, were bent over washing clothes in the river's edge. A few of them spoke to the two men in Spanish about other services they provided besides washing.

Ben tipped his hat and told them good-day, but he didn't fail to notice the embarrassment on Mark's face.

"Going into a new world. But take notice: There are folks down here would sell you for ten cents and kill you for the same amount."

Mark swallowed hard and nodded that he had heard his words of caution. They started up the narrow street, dodging noisy oxcarts. A young girl shouted to Mark from a balcony.

"Come up here and see me, gringo."

Mark glanced up, then ducked his head and tried not to look.

"She's just trying to make herself a living," Ben said, and booted the roan around a line of burros loaded with dead ironwood and mesquite sticks for firewood.

"Not from me," Mark managed.

"I know. We'll stable the horses ahead; then we can go find Señor Martinez, if he's in town."

"Good," the youth said, as if he were pleased by all the soliciting females.

Señor Martinez was a small man in a black suit with a pencil-thin mustache. A young woman in gauzy clothing sat upon his lap; she got up and bowed to them, then left.

"Have a seat, *mis amigos.*" He indicated the stuffed chairs across from his own.

"Good to see you. How is the cattle-selling business?" Ben asked settling into one chair, Mark in the other. "This is Mark, my man."

"Nice to meet you, Mark. Ah, the cattle business — she is very rough these days. Hard to find those big steers you want. A year ago I had many herds to sell; now I have few big cattle. But I can find smaller ones."

Ben shook his head — he needed the bigger ones to top the market in Kansas.

"In thirty days I can have you four hundred head here," Martinez said, pointing at the scarred tabletop with his index finger.

"How much per head?"

"Three dollars."

"No culls in them and I'll pay you two-fifty," Ben said, leaning forward toward the man to make his offer. When he finished he sat back.

"This girl, I think, wants to know if you want something to drink, Ben," Mark said.

"Tell her later," Ben said, wondering what Martinez would say to his counter-offer. That was fifty cents higher than they had spoken of in the fall. He'd promised him eight hundred head of big steers for two dollars, with delivery after Christmas and the New Year. Ben wanted to swear over not having done this buying sooner. Already news of the new Kansas market had reached the border and inflated the prices — but it was a long way to Kansas, and Martinez damn sure couldn't drive them up there. Ben doubted he could drive milk cows to a pen.

"Ah, *mi amigo,* you are so hard to trade with. I will lose much money on such a deal."

Ben reminded him of his promise.

"Ah, yes, but that was then and this is now, *mi amigo.*"

When would he have the other half of the herd he needed? He couldn't head out with only four hundred head and make any money for the risk and expenses he faced.

"When can you get me the rest?"

"I will scour the country for them. I will have the rest of them here at Aqua Fría by the first of February."

"Good," Ben said, and waved the bar girl over. "Bring us both beers and some food."

"What would you like to eat?" she asked.

He looked over at Mark. "Enchiladas, some beef?"

"Sure," he said.

"Bring us a nice platter of food," he said to her. She agreed and left them. "This is your son?" Martinez asked.

"No, he is my foreman."

"Ah, for such a young man he seems a good one."

Ben agreed with a nod. The first half of the herd would be there and ready to take north to his place in three weeks. He'd have to hire some help for the drive, which would take them ten days at least. It would be a good time to try out Hap's new wagon. Damn, he'd have to find some good mules to pull it too. Mexico was not the place to look — they had more hinnies than mules down there, and somehow claimed they were the same. Wrong — a hinny was not the same as a mule. A hinny was out of a stallion and a jenny, and never met the quality of a mule. No, he needed to find a Comanche to get him a real set of mules. They bred more of them than anyone save Missourians.

After they ate, Ben checked the two of

them into the hotel and they took their things to the room. He felt much better with half the deal he'd made. Surely Martinez could find him four hundred more big steers in forty-five days — it was the man's business.

"Are all these women in Mexico selling their bodies?" Mark asked when they were in bed with the lights out.

"No, you're in their district."

"Oh, then all Mexican women aren't . . . whores?"

"No."

"Good," Mark said, then rolled over, and their conversation was finished.

"There's some pretty ones, though, ain't there?" Ben asked, smiling at the ceiling in the room's darkness.

"There sure are."

"We've got to get up early and get back home."

"Sure, Ben."

They stopped in a crossroads store en route home. Ben ordered some crackers and cheese. While the clerk was wrapping the food, Ben looked outside and noticed three young men ride up. They looked tough enough and were confronting Mark, who had stayed outside with the horses.

39

When Ben saw one of them dismount and swagger toward Mark, he frowned, upset, and headed for the front door.

"Cowboy, you got a good roan horse there. I think I'll take him for myself." The other two smirkers sitting their horses laughed and egged on the one on the ground.

"Stay there unless you want to die," Mark said, holding his left hand out.

Ben stopped outside the doorway in the shadows of the porch and heard the boy's words issued to his challenger. He was impressed.

"You got a pistol, no?"

"Yeah, and don't ask me to use it," Mark said.

One of the young men sitting on the horses had noticed Ben, and cautioned the one on the ground in Spanish about the *"hombre grande"* on the porch. He glanced toward Ben and then back at Mark.

"So you win this time, gringo," he said, and turned.

"Wait," Mark said. "Let's finish this. Ben can watch your two *amigos* while you and I have it out. If I meet you again, I want you to think different than you do now."

"Ho, so you want to fight?" The challenger, a wiry youth, looked impressed.

"Yeah, I do." Mark hung the gun belt on

his saddle horn and took off his vest, then his shirt. "Let's see about this."

"Oh, you are going to take the whipping of your life."

"Same thing I think about you."

Ben moved out to the edge of the porch. He used a finger to wave the other two back away from the space in the mesquite, and after a scowl they did as he indicated.

The fight was on. Mark charged in fist swinging and landed one on his adversary's cheek. Then he took one to the right eye and gave a three-blow account that sent the Mexican staggering back. He recovered and closed in. It was blow for blow, and both fighters looked like tireless windmills.

But the battering they both were issuing made Ben think they were close to equally matched. Then Mark drove a hard uppercut and sent his opponent to the ground. Seated on his butt, the man shook his head. "What's your name, gringo?"

"Mark Fulton, why?"

" 'Cause I want to remember not to fight you again, Mark Fulton." He rubbed his jaw, shook his head, and never offered to get up.

"What's yours?" Mark extended a hand to help him up to his feet.

"Miguel Costa."

"Nice to meet you," Mark said as he swept up his felt hat and headed for the horse, reshaping the round crown as he went.

Ben handed him the reins to his horse and nodded.

Mark pursed his split lip and nodded back. They didn't need any words. The matter was handled; they started back to the MC.

"How far was I from needing to shoot him?" Mark asked as they rode up the wagon tracks in the brown grass that split the mesquite and greasewood.

"How far did you think?"

"I was watching the other two some and figured I'd never get all of them. But if you hadn't come out on the porch when you did I reckon I'da done it anyway."

"Good judgment," Ben said, and they began to trot their horses in the growing twilight.

" 'Cept I never shot a person before."

"Big difference."

"I figured so." They rode on and reached the home place after midnight.

Chapter 3

For three days Ben watched the clouds roll in off the faraway gulf, big, thick gray thunderheads full of needed winter moisture. Water would sure help lots of the winter oat crop shriveled up by the dry spell that had grasped the country for over six weeks. The drops pelted his slicker as he headed up the lane for the Basset place. Reo Basset had served in his outfit during the war — by the looks of his tumbledown place, he could use some wages.

"That you, Captain? Come in; my gawd, it's a bad day to be out on horseback." The whiskered face on the man looked unfamiliar, but it had been three years since he had split from Ben's outfit when they came back from the war.

He met Reo's new wife, a girl of fifteen, maybe, and pregnant. Ben had heard the man's first wife died the fall before of childbirth complications.

"I'm taking a herd to Kansas this spring. Wondered if you wanted to go along?" Ben asked.

Reo made a pained face. "Captain, I'd love to. But, you know, I couldn't hardly leave Flossy here all alone, new baby coming and all."

"I understand," Ben said, and rose. "I hate to run, but I need to make some tracks. If you reconsider, let me know."

"I sure will. You seen many of our old outfit lately, Captain?"

"Yes, I have. Seen John Thornton — he's got a bad leg, broke it in a horse wreck. Nile's got lung trouble. Morris Green — he's got a new wife, has to stay there 'cause she couldn't run the ranch by herself. Fact I've seen like near all of them in the past several days."

"Anyone from our old army bunch going with you?"

"One, Dru Nelson, said he'd go."

"Never remarried, did he?"

"No," Ben said. Nelson didn't have some child bride he had to stay home with and pat on the butt either.

"Easy enough for him to go," Reo said.

"I guess. Take care, soldier; I'll see you. Thanks, ma'am. Take care of him; he was a brave man in his company during the war."

"I sure will," she drawled like a person relieved of a big burden.

Who did he have who could work? Mark,

and Dru, the grouchiest man in his old outfit — that meant he needed to try Billy Jim Watts on the drive up from Mexico in a few weeks. *Try* was the word. Then he needed two more hands besides them. Where would he ever find them?

He checked the sun — damn, he had no time left to go home and clean up. Why, he'd have to run his roan to ever arrive at her place by a respectable time for supper. Why did he ever get so involved — Oh, well, he'd not disappoint her, and he put spurs to the horse's sides.

The last half mile he walked the hard-breathing roan to cool him. Twilight set in over the hill country; days were getting too short. Soon there'd be more darkness than daylight — he always hated this time of year. The closer he drew to her place the more antsy he felt about this entire thing of seeing her under her terms. But that was foolish — she'd only invited him to supper.

Of course, she no doubt by this time had seen that shiner on her son's eye. She'd probably give Ben a lecture over him letting her boy become a ruffian. Maybe he deserved a speech, too. And if Mark had worn that six-gun home . . . Probably he had; he never went without it — even to the outhouse, best Ben could tell.

Her dogs barked a welcome and she came to the open front door.

"Ben?" she called out as he dropped heavily from the saddle.

"It's me, ma'am." He loosened the cinch.

"I was worried you had work to do," she said, coming to meet him.

"I-I could have. But no, I was looking forward to your cooking."

"Good," she said, and stood before him looking fresh, her hair pinned up and curls spilling down the back of her head. Even in the dimness of twilight he could see she wore a new dress and he could smell the same perfume from the thank-you letter. Lavender was what it was. She fit her hand in the crook of his arm and led him toward the house.

"I'll get you some hot water for you to wash up with."

"Fine, I intended to go back —"

"Ben, you're a busy man with lots on your mind. I'm just pleased you could make it."

"Well, I could have done better. Finding hands is sure not easy."

She paused in the lighted doorway and turned back to look at him. "Why? I thought everyone needed work."

"Needing it and doing it are two different things." They both laughed aloud at his words.

She left him at the threshold and hurried inside for the hot water. He hung his hat on the peg and closed his dry eyes for a moment. Where would he find enough help? The issue had begun to niggle him and might soon fester.

"Hope it won't scald you," she said, pouring some steaming water in the washpan on the table.

"It's cool enough out here. Won't be long it will be just right," he said, rolling up his sleeves.

His hands and face washed and dried on the towel, he stepped over the threshold. The place looked spick-and-span. No boys? He wondered where the two younger ones were at. She smiled up at him and nodded for him to go to the table set for two while she fixed plates on a dry sink.

"Boys out?" he asked.

"They're spending the night at the Adamses'. Had something at church they wanted to attend and will be back in the morning."

"Fine, I just —"

"Sit down. I'll bring the food, and you don't need to stand up for that."

"I'd seat you." He showed her the chair he had ready for her.

She wrinkled her nose and shook her head

to dismiss his gentlemanly ways as unnecessary. "Be comfortable, Ben. I've got to get this and that."

"Fine." He took his place.

"Hope you like this," she said, putting a heaping plate before him.

"After eating Hap's food for so long, I suspect it will suit me fine." He looked over the homemade dumplings and chicken, and saliva began to flow in his mouth in anticipation. It had been ages since he had eaten any.

"You've done fine here," he said, indicating her spread on the table.

When she was ready to seat herself across from him, she folded her new dress under her and sat down. For a long moment their eyes met, and he felt the magnetism pull on his entire body.

"Guess we better eat before it gets cold," she said with a smile, and he agreed.

"Mark sure likes working for you," she said after a moment. "I hope you knowed that."

"I like him. He's making a man."

"I was kinda upset about the black eye. Not at you — I mean, I didn't want him going around looking for trouble, but he said it came looking for him and he settled it."

Ben finished chewing his mouthful and nodded. "He did it like a man. I never interfered. It was his thing; he resolved it."

"Kinda hard for me to be a father to boys. You know what I mean? I try not to be a busybody mother and . . ." She put down her fork on her plate and sighed. "I guess I'm just talking your ear off about my own business."

"No, Jenny, you talk; I'm listening. It would be hard being a single parent."

"Three boys don't put me on the most eligible list either."

"I'd think those strapping boys of yours would be an asset."

"Well, they ain't."

"You've done well with them."

"I hope so. I can see Tad wanting to do what Mark does, and he's only thirteen, and the ten-year-old, Ivory, is coming on strong. Why, they'd go to Kansas with you in a minute. But they're too young to drive cattle, I know."

"Hard to keep boys down on the farm." Ben laughed, and she did too.

After the meal for dessert she fed him two slabs of her pecan pie and hot coffee. Real coffee, too — strong and not like tea. Jenny knew how to make real coffee.

The candle in the reflector cast a flickering light. Outside, the wind picked up, and he figured a northern was blowing in — this close to the end of November, it was time for some frosty weather.

"Guess that north wind's going to blow the rain out," she said.

"Maybe, hoped all day for some."

Seated across from him, she wet her lips. "Ben, I made something for you. I-I didn't . . . I hope it won't embarrass you."

"Oh, you couldn't do anything to embarrass me."

"Close your eyes, then." She started to get up. "No peeking."

He shut his lids. She didn't have to get him anything. He heard her soles rush across the room and back.

"Stand up," she said, and he felt her guiding his hands into leather sleeves; then she put the garment upon his shoulders and he opened his eyes. He wore a buckskin shirt, complete with fringe.

She stepped before him, drew the front together and buttoned it, then stepped back. Her right hand over her mouth, her left hand holding that elbow, she looked hard at him. At last she nodded her head in approval. "I made some good guesses."

He walked around her great room, ran his palms over the sleeves, and nodded in approval. "You did wonderful. But you didn't —"

"Do you realize that you sent five deer over here for us to eat? That's where the buckskin came from. The boys and I tanned the hides."

"Take all five hides for one shirt?"

She made a face at him. "No, you want the rest?"

"No, no. I just wondered."

Then she was in his arms and he kissed her. It felt like the thing to do, what he wanted to do, and he closed his eyes to savor the sugar in her mouth. Then, when he figured he'd gone as far as he dared, he pulled back.

It felt comforting to have her clean-smelling hair in his face, her subtle body pressed to his. They stood and he rocked her back and forth. Why had he waited so long? He could have lost her with his stubborn waiting.

"I love the jacket. Almost too pretty to wear."

"No, you wear that to Kansas for good luck."

"It'll get all dusty, and the weather'll be bad — I don't want to ruin it."

"Nothing would make me prouder than to know that you wore it into Abilene."

"I will," he said, and swung her in his arms. "Jenny, you know if I can make this trip and things are as good as this colonel says they are, I'll own a spread big enough to support a wife."

She looked up at him. "You don't need a big spread —"

He put his fingertips on her lips. "I need a bigger spread. When I come home from Kansas . . ."

"Yes?"

"I'll ask you to marry me," he managed to get out in a hoarse whisper.

"Why not now and not worry about what my answer will be all the way up there and back?"

"Jenny Fulton, will you marry me?"

"Tomorrow or whenever — yes."

A load slipping from his shoulders, he hugged her so tight he feared he might crush her. "Well, damn. Now I've done it."

"You have." She nestled her face against his new shirt. "You don't regret it, do you?"

"No." He blew out a deep breath. "I may just fly to Kansas like a big eagle."

"When do I need my dress done?"

He looked at the underside of the shakes on the roof. The soonest he could get back would be August, and if they had any trouble it would be later. Damn — so much he didn't know about the land between up there and where he stood in her small house.

"If I can't be back by September I'll send word. But soon as I can . . ." He hugged her again. "What'll the boys think?"

"They'll get you on their side and it'll be four against one."

Ben shook his head. How long would he be up north? No way to know. He still had little help for the drive — that concerned him as much as anything. He'd need a larger house. Maybe he'd been foolish asking her? No, he felt good about that, even relieved that it was over and she'd agreed.

He reached in his vest pocket. "I about forgot. I don't have a ring, but I do have my grandmother's gold locket. You can wear it if you want to."

"Of course I want to," she said, and took it from him. With care she opened the latch and studied the faded tintypes. "That her and him?"

"Yes."

"Well, hook it on me."

"Jenny . . . Jenny, I'd love to."

Chapter 4

Mules! Mules! Ben had listened to enough from Hap about needing four stout jasshonkies to pull all that grub they'd need to take with them to ever reach Kansas. His head was rattling about it when he set out to find a half-breed Comanche horse and mule trader by the name of Rain Crow. Ben switched horses to ride that day, and instead of Roan, he'd saddled Tom Jack, a stout bay horse in his string.

The last he heard, Rain Crow, the trader, was hanging out around Gunderburg, a German community west of Ben's place. He left the ranch before the rain-soaked dawn appeared and under his yellow slicker struck the road west.

On a dreary early-December morning, only good thing was the falling rain. A man who made his living with grass and livestock never took rain lightly. Sometimes there might be too little, but in the hill country of west Texas there hardly ever was too much. Droplets pattered on his rubber slicker and felt hat as he put Tom Jack in a long trot. It would be past noon before he reached Gunderburg, and then he still needed to locate Rain Crow. A smile was on his lips. It was a fitting day to go look for the trader. If anyone knew where to find four good mules, the Comanche should, if they were in the country.

Past noontime he was at Sturdivan's Saloon with a schooner of dark beer, filling a small plate with food off the free lunch counter. The patter of rain drumming on the tin roof, Ben made himself at home.

"That hoss trader Rain Crow around town?" he asked the rotund man behind the bar.

"Yeah, I see him yesterday."

"Good, I need to talk to him. Where'll he be?"

"Down at the Alamo."

"Well, that place any better than before?" Ben knew the joint had several shootings and a few murders to its credit — though the bodies were usually dragged outside the building.

"Same one runs it as before. Big Louie."

Ben nodded that he'd heard the man. The best part about Sturdivan's table spread was the smoked sausages. He took several slices and crackers on his plate back to the bar to devour them.

"What you need to buy?" Sturdivan asked, polishing a beer schooner across the bar.

"Mules to pull a wagon."

The German shook his head. "I don't know where any are for sale, but that breed he can find 'em."

"Why I rode over here. Good sausage."

"My wife, she makes them."

"Tell her she's very good."

"You got a wife?"

Ben shook his head — he was working on one, but there was no sense telling the bar owner about her.

"I was going to get her recipe for your wife."

"Thanks anyway. I'll have to come back and see you to get some more."

"Good. You want more beer?"

"No, thanks, I better get over to the Alamo and find Rain Crow."

"You come back — I always have smoked sausage."

"I sure will. Thanks." He took the last of it from his plate in a sandwich between two crackers and headed for the door, eating as he went. There'd be lots of riffraff in the Alamo Saloon. He felt for his six-gun and hefted it in place under the slicker as he went outside. A spray of mist struck his face. He checked the girth and swung in the saddle.

The Alamo Saloon was under the hill on the banks of Nephi Creek. A set of hip-shot ponies lined the hitch rack when he topped the rise coming past the two-story stone mill building. He could hear the hiss of the steam engine that powered the flour mill when he dismounted and tied the reins on the rack. The Alamo's porch roof leaked when he stepped on the springy board floor and drew the unplaned wooden door back. The bat wings were tied open, and a haze of smoke clouded the room.

Conscious of the many hard looks following him, he went to the bar and ordered a beer. When the grizzle-faced bartender brought it, Ben paid him the dime and turned slow-like to consider the room's contents. Several toughs sat under the yellow light coming from some candle lamps around a wagon wheel hung from a rope off the ceiling. The end of the rope was tied off on the far wall.

"You here on business?" the bewhiskered bartender asked.

"Yeah," Ben said, not turning as he watched the progress of the card game. "I'm looking for Rain Crow."

"He ain't been in today. You got business with him?"

"Yeah," Ben said, sucking on his tongue trying to dislodge a small piece of sausage caught in his teeth. "Working on a trade. Tell him Ben McCollough's in town."

"May not see him for weeks."

"Tell him when you see him. He knows me."

"You might be the damn law."

"Just tell him," Ben said, hearing the edge of impatience rising in his words.

He finished the beer and set the mug on the bar.

Ben reset the rain-sodden hat on his head and started for the door. Something clawed at his guts. Something was amiss in this dive. He felt it, knew something was wrong; then he noticed someone step away from the bar, throw his shoulders back, and start to bar his way.

"Stranger, what the hell you doing in this place, anyway?" the drunk demanded, wavering on his boot heels and blocking Ben's exit.

"For me to know and you to find out." Ben caught him by the front of his shirt and tossed him hard enough against the bar that the man grunted when he hit and slid down to the brass rail. Ben's fist closed on the redwood butt of his navy .44; when he spun around, the long Colt filled his hand.

"Anyone else in here want to know?" The loudest sound was his breath rushing up into his nose. Not even a glass tinkled. All eyes were on him, including those of a few dull-looking doves with low-cut blouses and stringy hair.

"Guess that settled that," one of the women said. "Damn, mister, you sure threw him away." She came striding over with her hands on her hips and wagging her way over until she stood ten feet away from him. "These others damn sure don't want any part of you."

Her words brought a titter from the crowd.

"Good," Ben said, then spun on his heel and started to go outside. The drunk on the floor made a grab for him. Too slow — Ben whacked him with the barrel of his pistol and he fell back on the floor. After a quick check of the others, he saw no opposition, and went out the door.

He holstered the Colt and gathered his reins as the water began to run off his hat brim again. His attention centered on the rough board door — no one came after him.

He put the horse in the livery — it was already late afternoon and there was no sign of the Comanche breed. His trip might be in vain — no telling where Rain Crow was. Word would get to him soon enough. Ben took his own bedroll and saddlebags over his shoulder and went three doors down to check into the Crockett Hotel.

Piling his things in the bedroom, he went back downstairs to the lobby. After explaining to the clerk a man might seek him, he went across to Sturdivan's Saloon and joined a low-stakes poker game. Introducing himself to the four men, he anted up a quarter and waited for his cards.

A barber named Grandstein, a thin-faced man named Vogelman, and a quick-eyed boy by the name of Delf were the other players. The game proceeded. Ben held two pairs and when the hand was over he won.

"Just beginner's luck," Vogelman said, and began to shuffle the cards.

Ben had taken a chair with his back to the side wall, where he could see the entrance and most of the room. The cards came again; he held an ace and drew three sevens.

Bets were laid down and he won the second hand. Vogelman frowned and cleared his throat when Ben raked in his winnings. But cards, like some women Ben knew, could turn south as fast as they came right in a legit game. The barber won next and looked relieved hauling in his winnings. Four years of gambling with other officers taught Ben a lot about poker — but his real lessons came watching the enlisted men play. He could spot clumsy card shifts and sleeve stuffing — marked cards so you could tell what your opponent held.

"Where's your place?" Vogelman asked, looking over the pasteboards fanned out in his hand.

"Teeville," Ben said, disappointed in his cards and undecided whether to simply fold or try for a good draw.

Vogelman nodded.

Ben looked up when someone came inside: bareheaded, with lots of gray showing in his braided hair, the unmistakable high cheekbones on a swarthy face. Rain Crow had arrived. He spotted Ben and like a cat crossed the saloon's sawdust floor. He squatted down close by Ben's chair and put his back to the grooved board wall.

"They say you need to see me, big Ben."

"Need four good mules," Ben said, tossing in his hand.

"Meet you daybreak, down by the creek."

"They broke?"

Rain Crow shook his head so his shoulder-length braids danced on the shoulders of his faded flannel shirt. For a long moment Ben considered — four un-broken mules. Did he have the time or the patience to mess with them? If they could use a team of horses to go to Mexico and get the first steers, they wouldn't need that many supplies in the wagon for that weeklong or so drive.

"How much?"

"Forty apiece."

"Too much."

"They good mules."

"But they ain't broke."

"You see they good mules."

"You in?" the barber asked; it was his turn to deal.

"Leave me out this hand," Ben said, and turned back to Rain Crow. "I'll be there."

The Indian nodded, straightened, and headed for the door under the disapproving eyes of the other customers.

"Next time you do business with that blanket-ass sumbitch, do it somewheres else," Vogelman said, arranging his new hand.

"There was a time I'da backhanded you out of that chair. I'll just say I didn't hear you," Ben said, and nodded at the man.

"Well, guess you're a damn Injun lover."

A smile split Ben's lips. "It's over, stupid. He's left."

"It may be over for you, but them damn Comanches are still out there killing folks west of here."

"Rain Crow's been around here all his life. He ever offer to kill you?"

"No, but he's a damn half-breed, acts and looks like them woman-raping, baby-killing sons a bitches."

"Let's drop it," Ben said.

Vogelman looked over at him, appraised his large frame, and nodded in agreement. The game continued until Ben grew weary and excused himself, some fifteen dollars richer.

The hotel bed offered little solace. Ben's concerns ran from his new commitment to Jenny Fulton to Martinez's failure to supply enough steers and the four unbroken mules. Things he must resolve came first — but thoughts of Jenny as his future wife filtered through the rest like smoke at a barbecue.

He woke up bleary-eyed, dressed, and looked out the window at the predawn darkness. Maybe he had time for some coffee and a bite to eat. Rain Crow would be there whenever he got there. Amazing how a half-breed could do math as well as that one. The story about the horse trader was that his mother had been rescued from a tribe of Comanches by Texas Rangers when he was six years old. She stayed with her white relatives; he ran off and rejoined his father's people. When he was taken prisoner and brought back as a teen, he moved in with her. Both she and the boy lived at the edge of white society. Taken captive at fourteen, her face tattooed, and so many Indian ways about her, white people ignored her. They also shunned the half-breed son, except for his white grandfather, who taught Rain Crow all he knew about money and horses.

The coffee, ham, bread, and eggs at the café helped Ben's disposition. He retrieved his horse from the livery. In the cool north wind that swept the land and had chased away the rain, he used his bedroll blanket for a coat. Tom Jack acted ready to buck, and he kept him in close check heading down the empty street for the creek.

Somewhere off in the distance he heard a jackass bray, no doubt one of his mules. Ben shook his head, then felt the horse underneath him gather up again. Ready to release the blanket and pull leather, he knew the grain-fed bay could turn things into a high-jumping contest in a split second. But talking softly, he quieted him and headed downhill toward the creek.

In the first shafts of sunup, he saw the four mules, which raised their heads and brayed in a chorus at him. Not bad-sized mules, twelve to thirteen hands tall, two blacks, a sorrel, and one paint. He wished they'd all been solid colors, but Indian mares a spotted one was bound to show up.

Under a blanket, Rain Crow squatted close to a large cedar. A repeating rifle across his lap, he nodded when Ben rode up.

"I don't like the spotted one," Ben said, dismounting and dropping the reins so Tom Jack was ground-tied.

"He's sound." The breed gave a "no matter" look.

"Yeah, but he's a flag. I don't need a flag where I'm going."

"Only mules I have. Hard to find good ones."

Ben dropped down and squatted beside him. He drew the blanket up over his shoulder. In the shade it was still cool.

"They threes and fours."

"Will they lead?"

Rain Crow nodded. "Plenty good lead."

"Bottom dollar."

"Hundred-fifty."

"Hundred."

"No!" The breed shook his head. "Have to go way west trade with crazy ones. Take lots of goods to get them. Have to dodge army now, too. No like me trade with *Itaha*."

Itaha meant "the people." Comanches called themselves by that name. Ben considered the mules. They would be as Rain Crow said, sound, and their ages would be right. But he dreaded the breaking process that lay ahead for him and his crew if he bought them.

"A hundred and twenty."

"No."

"A hundred-thirty." Ben shook his head warily. "That's more than anyone would pay for four wild mules."

"Good ones hard to find. You go up the trail with cattle?" He motioned to the north.

Ben nodded.

"You want horses too?"

"I could use some."

"Bring you forty head. No colts. Two hundred dollars. You pick out any bad ones."

Forty head plus the ones at the ranch would make a good-sized cavvy. He considered the offer — if Martinez got off his butt and found the rest of the cattle, he'd be in the market for horses.

"Some be broke; you like 'em, big Ben."

"Not stolen?"

"No, only Indian brands."

66

"Bottom dollar on these mules?"

"You take horses?"

Ben nodded, knowing Crow wanted to sell the horse herd, too.

"One hundred-thirty to you, big Ben."

"We'll trade, but you've got to be sure I get headed home with them."

Rain Crow smiled. "Me help. When you want horses?"

"This week sometime?" Ben dug out his purse and counted out the money in gold coins for the mules. He might be home by dark — if he was lucky — though he considered anything happening in the company of the mules could not be counted upon.

"Bring them in three days," Rain Crow said, and stood up. "You like horses plenty good."

"I like solid-colored horses."

"Horses be plenty good."

Damn, Ben knew by those words that he'd get some paints in whatever the trader delivered. Oh, well, he'd have his cow ponies. Might be a good market for them in Kansas after the drive. He could hope so, anyway.

Tom Jack gave the mules a wide-eyed look when Ben drove him in close. Rain Crow began bringing them over. He hitched the outside mule to the lead one's halter and did the same on the other side. So Ben had two leads wrapped around his saddle horn, a pair of mules on each side, and a goosey Tom Jack underneath him.

With care, he nudged the bay forward. The next thirty seconds would tell. Tom Jack blowing roller out his flared nostrils. Ben could feel the muscles down the horse's loin gathering under the saddle. He talked quickly and softly to the big horse in the midst of the canary-braying contest. One step, two . . . He checked him, and in a few more they were headed east in a rough trot, with Rain Crow on his own black horse riding beside them.

"What's Kansas like?"

"They say tall grass as far as you can see. Want to go along?"

"No, just wonder. How many more going?"

"There's talk all over about many folks taking herds up there."

"Them need more mules," Rain Crow said, as if thinking out loud.

"Before springtime you might do a lively business."

The breed nodded and rode in to lash the laggard black mule on the butt with his quirt.

"You going back to trade for some more?"

"Yes. You watch out, big Ben. That one you tossed aside last night, him bad one. Talk about shooting you."

"What's his name?"

"Harold Coulter. He plenty bad *hombre*."

"I'll watch for him. Thanks." Rain Crow wasn't afraid of much; when he said that Coulter was bad, he was that way.

Damned braying jackasses — he'd be glad to finally be home.

Chapter 5

Ben came out on the porch and met the glowing face of Billy Jim Watts. It looked like the boy had scrubbed until every freckle shone. He stood with his hat in his hand and the slab-sided horse snorting in the dust at his back.

"Morning. I heard you still lacked a crew, Mr. Ben."

"Billy Jim. Didn't I tell you —"

"Yes, sir, you said it would be pure hell most of the time. Still, I done considered all you said and I still want to work for you. You give me a chance — I'll work for free. I don't make a hand you can send me packing."

"It won't be no Sunday-school picnic. In fact, I'd bet my best horse before we get to the Indian Nation, you'll want to go back home."

Billy Jim stuck out his chest. "You got to be a man sometime."

The boy hit a chord. Only Ben hated to wet-nurse one to get him there. Dang — no

70

more men that he could hire. Maybe Billy Jim would be his best — No, not his best, but his only choice.

"Got all your stuff?"

"You mean I'm hired?"

"Trial basis only. We're breaking mules today. You hear them canaries?"

"Huh?" The youth made a face, then smiled. "You mean jackasses."

"That's it, and we have four unbroken ones to start with. Put that horse up. You can take him back home Sunday. Get down there and help Mark halter them."

"Yes, sir."

Ben looked up and frowned at the sight of a stranger. Aboard a small gray burro with his bare feet hanging out of ragged overalls came a black boy.

"Mr. Ben McCollough, sir," the youth called out, and bounded off the donkey's back.

"Yes?"

"My name's Digger Jones. I done heard you was needing help."

"Where you from, Digger?"

"From my mama, I guess."

"No." Ben chuckled. "I mean, where did you live last?"

"Oh, Mr. Jones's place up by San Antonio. But he don't got no more work."

"How old are you?"

"I says sixteen, maybe mores, maybe less."

"You ride and rope?"

"I sure does."

That was all he needed — a round- bottomed boy and a cotton-patch black one. He'd be lucky to ever get to Kansas. Digger Jones . . . Ben shook his head.

"Tell you what, Jones. I'm going to give you a try. You don't cut it, you'll have to move on. This is a man's work, and I pay a man's pay regardless of your skin color, but you better give me your all."

"What you got for me to do?"

"Mule breaking starts in a few minutes down at the corral. Wait," Ben said. "When did you eat last?"

"Two, three days ago."

Ben drew in a deep breath and shook his head. No way anyone could work who hadn't eaten since then. "Go in there and tell Hap I said to feed you."

"Yes, sah." A smile swept his dark face.

"Wait. What're you going to do with that burro?"

"Nothing. Turn him loose." Digger shrugged. "I's just found him to ride out here."

Ben nodded that he heard. One more

braying devil wouldn't hurt, he guessed. Then he frowned as the boy started around the house. "Where you going?"

"Around to the back door."

"No, go in the front door like the rest of the crew."

"You sure?"

"Yes. If you're going to be part of us, then you eat and sleep with us."

Digger shook his head, as if taken aback. He blinked his dark eyes. "I make you a hand, Mr. Ben, I sure will."

Good, he'd need lots of hands. He'd better go see what Mark and Billy Jim were doing with the mules. He glanced back at the house. No sounds, so Hap hadn't killed his latest employee; maybe he'd even fed him. Two or three days since he'd eaten . . . He scowled at the burro over by the corrals grazing like he owned the place. Three boys and one grown man hired. Dru Nelson wasn't supposed to show up until the next week, when Ben hoped to go to the border for half of the herd.

The mules came next, and he set out for the breaking pen.

On the end of a lead rope with both heels plowing up mud and manure, Billy Jim was hanging on to his mule. A little red-faced, he showed no signs of quitting the process.

The wide-eyed animal in the lead acted like the devil himself were on his heels, and he was churning up ground with his hooves to escape the boy on behind him. Ben wanted to laugh, but he knew how serious this matter was for Billy Jim. He swung over the fence and headed off the walleyed one, caught the halter, and jerked the mule to a halt.

"I'm coming, Ben; don't let loose," Billy Jim shouted.

When Ben turned enough to see his new employee running for all he was worth, he wanted to shout. But it was too late — the mule reached out and cow-kicked the youth in the stomach and sent him sprawling on his butt.

Red-faced and angry, holding his belly with one hand, Billy Jim got up and took the halter from Ben. His eyes drawn into a squint, he held his fist up to show the mule how mad he'd made him.

"What we calling him?" Ben asked, gathering up the lead.

"How about Kicking Chicken?"

"Suits him," Ben said, and they moved aside as Mark's mule made a wide sweep around the pen.

Snubbed to the post in the center of the pen, Mark kept drawing in his slack to get the other black mule up against it.

When the mule went by again, Ben clapped his hands. The mule flew forward and Mark took up slack in the rope and had him tight to the post, the animal's mouth open wide, his wide-open yellow teeth popping only inches from Mark's shoulder.

"What are you calling him?" Ben asked, the shocked-faced Mark still giving the mule a berth.

"Nasty."

"Should I tie mine up too?" Billy Jim asked.

"Wouldn't hurt." Ben turned as Jones climbed up the fence and surveyed the mule operation.

"Boys, meet Digger. He's part of this crew now. Digger, you know about mules?"

"Yes, sah, Mr. Ben, they kicks and they bites and they tries to get ya."

"We learned that already. You want to try your hand at roping one?" He was anxious to see how well Digger could rope.

"I sure try."

"Lariat's on that post. We have those two left." Ben indicated the sorrel and the paint hiding in the corner. Digger strode across the corral and took down the rope, a shirtless black boy in wash-worn bib overalls. Ben tried not to have any preconceived

75

notions, but an ex-slave from the cotton patch . . . How could he know anything about a lariat? But Ben saw him string out a loop and start in a slow run parallel to the red mule — then he watched the lariat snake out and saw the youth's skills. Digger jerked slack and the loop caught close to the mule's throat.

Impressed, Ben hurried in to help him contain the animal.

"Wow!" Billy Jim shouted. "Where did you learn to do that?"

"A Messican fellow. Benito Pasquel. He taught me how."

"Damn, Digger, can you do that again?" Mark asked.

"I's sure can try." He finished wrapping his rope around the other snubbing post and dodged Red's hind kicks.

"What we calling him?" Ben asked.

"Him the Red Devil."

Ben agreed and Mark tossed Digger the second rope. He fashioned a loop and in seconds was circling with the paint running stiff-legged around the pen's perimeter. Out went the loop and Digger jerked his slake. The spotted mule was captured, and the other two boys ran in to help him contain the last one.

"What do we do next, Ben?" Mark asked.

"You going to drive them, Mr. Ben?" asked Digger.

"Yes, they're going to haul our cook's supply wagon to Kansas."

"Then let's harness them, and puts them puppies on a drag. Them two can be my outriders and snub them. I can sure drive them," Digger said.

"They're green as grass." Ben looked skeptical at his latest employee's ambitious plans.

"That's how we did it where I was raised."

"We'll leave them tied and go find enough posts to make a drag," Ben said, with little doubt that Digger knew more about breaking mules than the other three of them combined.

The mules were hooked four abreast. Billy James on the buckskin mare snubbed the paint that Digger harnessed on the left, then Red, then Chicken and Nasty on the right side snubbed to Tom Jack and Mark in the saddle.

Digger held the reins, telling Ben to hook them up from behind the drag of poles they had roped together, in case they jerked forward and pulled the poles over on top of him.

His teamster, with the lines thrown over

his shoulder, nodded when Ben backed away. "They're hitched."

"Good, you boys step forward when I's cluck at them. Not fast. Not fast. These here mules gonna wanta to leave this place when they finds these here logs be chasing them."

Digger clucked and gave a wave of the lines. Red went sky-high on his hind feet. Billy Jim took a new wrap on his lead and stopped the paint from acting up. Rearing on their hind feet, wildly braying, the mules headed for the open pasture, Digger half running, holding back on the lines and the lead ponies containing them, along with the drag.

"Not half-bad. Not half-bad, for the first time," Hap said, smiling after them.

"But they sure ain't ready for Mexico," Ben said, and headed for the shed.

"Where you going, Cap?"

"To buy me two more pistols. Don't think the last two I hired have any of their own."

"Well, if Billy Jim don't shoot himself in the foot, you'll be lucky, and does that mule skinner really need one?" Hap frowned like he disapproved arming any former slave.

"I think so. He's got to defend this outfit if we come under attack."

"Yeah, but that's different."

"When fifty Indians jump us up in the Nation, you're going to say, 'I wish that Ben had taught them boys how to shoot.' "

"You win. How long you want them mules drove?"

"All day."

"That'll unkink their tails some," Hap agreed, and fell in with his stiff-legged walk, throwing the right leg ahead and catching up with it.

"We need two more cowboys."

"You think them three are going to work out?"

"They'll have to."

"None of them soldiers that was with us —"

"That was with us. No, they've got wives and families, and they don't want to go fight Injuns and jayhawkers. Their fighting days are over, Hap."

"Then why are we going?"

"I aim to make enough money to quadruple the size of this ranch."

"What if you don't make that much?"

"May have to go again. But I ain't planning on it."

"I can see us now, spending the rest of our lives traipsing up and down this trail Colonel McCoy is laying out."

"You know my uncle went to California

in the Gold Rush. He came back with enough gold to buy a big plantation. Others, they came back broke and worn out. I intend to come back from Kansas with enough to buy me a much bigger place or more land."

Hap jerked off his weathered hat and scratched his thin pate. "Cap'n, when you set your mind you're a tough man to divert. Like getting that black boy a pistol — weren't no sense in arguing."

Ben clapped him on the shoulder. "Hap, we're going to do it."

"Don't doubt it in the least. You got another straggler up by the corral. You see him?"

Ben nodded. This one was older, maybe past twenty. He wore a six-gun and a flat-crowned black hat cocked back on his head so his curly dark brown hair showed. He wore a snow-white shirt and leather vest, as well as leather cuffs. The blue silk bandanna around his neck must have cost five dollars.

"You Mr. McCollough?"

"Yes," he said, and stopped to appraise the new arrival.

"Chip Fields, my name. They said in Teeville you were looking for drovers for a drive north."

"You been up the trail before, Chip?"

"Ah, no, sir. But I can find my way around good."

"Where've you worked?"

"I was raised on a ranch west of Fort Worth."

Ben knew the clothes this one wore were never purchased on cowpuncher's wages. "Where else?"

"I was in the rangers for eighteen months."

"You retire?"

"Kind of, but I don't know what my rangering's got to do with —"

"Driving cattle."

"Yeah, driving cattle. I can rope fair enough, ride, and you hiring hands or not?"

Ben looked pained at him. Something was wrong here. He was too fancily dressed, for one thing. He sure might not fit in well with his boys. He had an attitude problem for Ben's part.

"Mr. McCollough, I need work."

"I need help, but I can't see you fitting in very well with my crew. They're some good ranch boys — obviously they ain't seen all the bright lights you have. But being on a drive like this you have to be like a family and all pull the same load."

"I'll pull my share, and any more that's needed."

"That's what bothers me. What happened to you and the rangers?"

"I shot a man who I thought had a gun."

"What did he have?"

"He was going after a letter from some legislator. I thought he was after a shoulder holster."

"That's your story?"

"Honest to God." He raised his right hand in an oath.

"All right, but don't go to lording it over the others — including the black."

"You gotta black cowboy?"

"That not fit you? Yes, I do, and if you can outrope him, I'd like to see it."

"Yes, sir. Where are they?"

"Out breaking mules. They'll be back by dark, or the mules will be, anyway. Just remember — I won't warn you; you aren't their boss." Ben pointed his finger at his own chest. "I'm the boss."

"Yes, sir. What should I do today?"

"Put on some working clothes and replace the weak poles alongside the squeeze chute runway. I don't want these new cattle laying it down when we road-brand them."

"Yes, sir."

"Hap will show you where the diggers are at. Set them at least three feet in the ground and tamp them in."

"Yes, sir."

Ben went and caught the gray horse, called Chief. This crew business got tougher and tougher. If he didn't have trouble with Fields before they got to the Red River, he'd buy himself a new hat in Abilene. He'd better like his old one that he cocked back on his head and then threaded in the latigos on the girth. He talked to Chief to set him at ease, then swung into the saddle and headed for town. In three days or so they were heading for Mexico to get the first round of cattle — half a herd. It bothered him that Martinez might be playing tricks on him to get higher prices now that this new interest in cattle had shown up on the border.

In the gun shop, he purchased five used revolvers and put in an order for a half dozen new Spencer rifles, five thousand rounds of ammo, and plenty of tubes. The .50-caliber Spencer with its tube-feeding system was much more reliable than the Henry Winchester. The brass works in the Henry were subject to wear in a hurry — couple hundred rounds shot through them and they really were worn out.

The rim-fire .50-caliber ammo for the Spencer wasn't the greatest, but it gave lots of firepower in the hands of a few men. He conversed for an hour and a half with the gunsmith, Bill Jenkins. Then he had a beer and counter lunch next door. The handguns in a tow sack tied to his saddle horn, he ducked in the mercantile and spoke to Mrs. Whitaker about material. He ended up buying a bolt of deep blue cotton, and when she poked around about why he needed it, he only smiled and said, "For a project."

Outside on the boardwalk, a boy pushed off from where he stood against the side of the store and hurried over. He wore a straw sombrero on his back held by the string at his throat.

"Señor McCollough?"

He looked hard and recognized Miguel Costa from the fistfight. "You're a long ways from home."

"I hear you need cowboys."

"Who told you that?"

"Rex Ford, he say you asked him to ride to Kansas."

"How do you know Rex Ford?" Rex was a former member of his company in the war, one of his exes. He'd ridden by and asked Rex to join him.

"He's married to my cousin."

"Rex Ford send you?"

Costa blinked his brown eyes in question.

84

"No, he say you hiring."

"I don't hire troublemakers."

"I no make trouble. I make you good cowboy."

With the flat part of his thumb, Ben cleaned the grit from the corners of his mouth and considered the youth. Every kid in Texas needed work, and he couldn't seem to hire a grown-up.

"Be out at the MC in the morning. You're on trial. But if you cause any trouble, I'll fire you in a minute."

"*Sí, señor. Gracias.*"

He watched the boy run off between the two buildings. What did he ride, a burro too? That confounded thing Digger rode in on was still grazing around the house when he left. Maybe one of Jenny's boys would want it to ride. He'd ask — then he recalled the purchase of the bolt of material underneath his arm.

He'd better set up some credit at the store for her, too, before he left for Kansas — in case she needed something. He scratched his left ear. This taking a woman was serious business. Lots he knew, and plenty more he didn't know about females. He almost wished he were coming back from Kansas and not just about to go. In all his planning for the drive he felt certain that he'd have those seasoned veterans he knew so well with him to meet the trail problems — not green recruits.

He undid the reins and swung into the saddle. Delivering the material and seeing Jenny was next on his list. Why did his stomach churn so at the prospect? No telling. He booted the gray and headed north in a long trot. It would be good to see her — somehow this courting had him feeling like an inexperienced schoolboy. Lord help him, he had a ranch full of them.

Over the last ridge, he dropped down the slope for her place. The dried grass made a ribbon between the wagon tracks. There was not much traffic. Of course, as meager as her living must be, she didn't have to run back and forth to town and outfit a crew either.

It would be different having a woman in his house. He'd not broached the subject to Hap yet either — for that his conscience niggled him. With no plans to run Hap off, he'd have to handle this whole matter with kid gloves. One more thing to fret about. His life was getting more complicated than all his problems as company commander had ever been during the war.

"Ben's here, Maw," Tad, the thirteen-year-old, shouted.

The stock dogs barked and wagged their tails.

"You got Mark working hard, Mr. Ben?" Tad asked.

"Yeah, he and the boys are breaking mules today."

"Breaking mules? You gonna plant cotton?"

"No," Ben said, dismounting. "Hap needs them to pull his supply wagon."

"Tad," Jenny said from the door, "Ben don't need to answer a million questions. Good to see you. What brings you over?"

"Oh, I brought you this." He held out the bolt to her.

She looked speechless and blinked at him. Then she sniffled and turned away. Was she about to cry? He'd only brought her a bolt of material; he'd no idea how much cloth was on it or how much it took to sew a dress.

"It's sure pretty material," she said, hugging it.

"Just blue material," he said, feeling awkward about the whole thing.

"Come in. You must be starved. We've got brown beans." She took him by the arm and he spoke to her ten-year-old, Ivory, coming inside. After she seated him, she carefully put the bolt on the bed's quilt top, still looking very impressed with the gift.

"Come on, Ivory, we've got cows to milk," Tad said.

"Huh? Oh, yeah. Good to see you, Mr. Ben." And the barefoot boy beat a tattoo on the worn floor as he headed out after his bucket-carrying brother.

Jenny brought Ben a bowl of beans and a spoon. When she bent over to set it down, he saw a tear coming down her cheek. With the side of his finger he caught it and looked deeply into her eyes. He had never come to upset her or show off. It was just a bolt of blue cloth.

"Will it make the dress you want?"

She closed her eyes and then gave him a peck on the cheek. "That and shirts for my boys and even curtains. You know how much material is on a bolt like that?"

"No, ma'am, but if you get all that from it, it'll be cheap enough." She made a good show; he decided that things were even closer at her house than he had imagined.

"We've been talking," she said, going for the coffeepot. "The boys and I . . . could we watch your place while you're gone to Kansas?"

"Sure going to need someone to do that. Yes, I'd say you could. Would twenty and food be enough?"

"Enough? Why, Ben —"

"Hey." He stood up. She put the coffeepot on the table and fell into his arms.

"Oh, I hate so to beg."

"You aren't begging. When I come back you'll be my wife; it'll be half yours." He patted her. Damn, he felt so weak holding her and still so strong. For a long moment he closed his eyes. Maybe when he returned he could live a real life with her. God, he hoped so.

Chapter 6

They were there in the morning when Ben opened the front door, ducked under the lintel to go out, and stretched his arms. A herd of horses were down by the creek, whining to his ranch stock. Rain Crow had delivered them. No telling about an Indian; he must have come in during the night sometime.

"Rain Crow's here with those horses," he said over his shoulder to Hap, who was busy rounding up breakfast for his crew.

"Figures," Hap said from the doorway. Then, shaking his head, he went back inside to tend his pots and pans.

"What's happening, Ben?" Mark asked, looking bleary-eyed coming from the bunkhouse.

"The horses arrived. They're down by the creek."

"Yeah, I can see them. They going to be as wild as those mules?"

"I sure hope not."

"Man, those dudes never give up. You

can work them all day and they'll still kick or bite you."

"They getting any better?"

"Sure, Digger can turn them in a forty-acre patch. All they wanted to do that first day was run away." Mark used his hands to shield his eyes from the spears of golden sunlight coming over the ridge. "Do we have to break them horses before we go to Mexico?"

"No, the ranch horses should be enough for that operation. We can take a little feed along too. We'll have room in the wagon for some grain that we won't have going to Kansas."

"Ben, can you advance Digger some money for a few clothes?" Mark asked.

"Guess I better if he's going to be part of this outfit."

Mark nodded as if in deep thought. "He's tougher than a tree knot. Hear him? He's around back right now chopping stove wood for Hap."

"He sure wants to do his part. And he can rope," Ben said, adding that he'd find him some duds.

"Yeah, I never would have believed that. His loops float out there so easy and land like bullets."

"They sure do. Get the rest of them up;

we've got to pick and choose horses after breakfast. Then saddle a horse and go down there and tell Rain Crow that he and whoever's with him can come eat."

"Yes, sir."

"Morning," Ben said, inside sipping his coffee when Digger came in with an armload of freshly split stove wood.

"Morning, Mr. Ben. Them hosses ours that I been hearing?"

"Yeah, Rain Crow brought them. We've got to pick out forty head for the trip and get them broke before we go to Kansas."

"Lordy," Digger said, dumping his armload in the box by the range. "Mules, horses to break. Why, this place'll sure be hopping."

"How much longer we need to snub them mules to a horse?"

"A few more days. Them mules, they ain't lost that booger edge yet."

Ben smiled. "We sure need that booger edge off them before we leave on the drive."

"Damn right you do, if you want me to cook ya food. Where's the rest of this outfit? Laying up? This ain't Sunday," Hap shouted, handing Digger a platter of bacon and eggs to set out.

"I don't know how many Rain Crow has

with him, or if they'll come, but I sent Mark to invite him."

"Hell, he may have a whole tribe with him. I'll watch and make some more if'n I get low. These boys eat like lions and tigers as it is."

Billy Jim came through the doorway, his face gleaming. Miguel came next, and the sleepy-eyed Chip last.

"You boys better get used to this. On the trail we'll get up before daybreak," Hap warned, rattling pans on the range.

"I can hardly wait," Chip mumbled as Billy Jim carried on a conversation with Hap.

Ben got up and went for more coffee. He turned when he heard someone at the door. "Come in, Rain Crow. See you got here."

The boys' heads all swiveled around to look at the hatless breed.

"Big Ben, bring you plenty good horses."

"Are they broke?" Chip asked.

The breed shook his head. Everyone laughed.

No, they weren't broken, and they'd dust down some of his cowboys before they were broken to ride. He hoped he had no wrecks. No way he could afford to lose any of them, as shorthanded as he felt. The vapors off the hot coffee softened the whiskers around his mouth as he chewed on his lower lip. Where to start first?

Forty head of bangtails were selected from the fifty-some the breed trader brought. Their tails all brushed the ground, and he knew that his cowboys would soon use their pocketknives to whittle them off. Mostly he had bays, with a couple of sorrels, a few roans, three mousy-colored ones, two striped zebra duns, and three paints.

They were selected, then the rest turned out for Rain Crow and the two Indian boys with him to take with them. Ben paid the breed his money and thanked him.

"Ben, you see . . . one from the saloon?" Rain Crow asked.

"No, why?"

"Someone say he looking for you."

"Thanks. I ain't hard to find."

"He's a Coulter. Harold Coulter. He's a bad one. You watch for him."

"I will, and thanks for bringing the horses." Rain Crow wasn't afraid of much — he sounded like he had respect for this Coulter.

"You have big time going to Kansas." Rain Crow grinned. "Say they have prettiest whores in all the world up there."

"And the ugliest ones too, I'd bet."

"Yeah, them, too." Rain Crow chuckled, waved, and rode after his herders.

The crew gathered up at the pens and sat on the ground or squatted down to wait his words. Ben considered what must be done next. "Digger, you and Billy Jim are assigned to the mules. Drive them some more."

The two nodded, got to their feet, and went for the pen that held the braying mules.

"We'll need a good fire started and the branding irons from the shed. The rest of us will be branding horses. Miguel, you build the fire. Chip will be in charge of the ropes. Any questions?"

They shook their heads, got up, and brushed off the seats of their pants to get ready to work. Things began to hop.

Soon Miguel had the mesquite and oak ablaze. Chip swung the rope over his head after they cut down to four horses in the sorting pen. Mark fussed over getting the irons hot enough in the fire. Ben and Miguel were soon working manila lariats, tossing loops and recoiling them. The four horses backed into a corner and were all wary-eyed at the strange things happening.

"These come from the Comanches?"

Chip asked, firing a noose at one of the ponies. The rope hit the animal's neck on the side, causing him to duck.

"We ready to catch one?" Miguel asked.

Ben nodded, and without effort the Mexican youth noosed one, caught the slack, and in a rip back on the slack, tightened it on the horse's throat.

Ben stepped in and gripped the rope, setting his boot heels in the dirt and fighting his way to the head slinger. Soon he threw his arms around the pony's neck and it made three diving steps, but Ben's weight soon stopped that action and the horse tried to back up. The animal's butt hit the fence and Miguel caught his front legs. Both boys hauled back and tripped the horse until Ben was on his butt, holding the animal's head.

Then Mark and Chip tied three of his legs with a shorter hank of rope. The bay pony blew rollers out his nose and rose up, trying to see. Ben sat on his shoulder to watch Mark indicate the bay's right hip with the smoking hot iron in his hands.

"That's the place."

A puff of stinking hair and burning smoke, and Mark rose up. "Look all right?"

"Looks like saddle leather. That should work." Ben undid the lariat around the pony's neck. "That went smooth enough.

Let's do the next one. Tail him up."

The next one Chip roped, and when the rope went tight, the horse stopped trembling. Miguel went up the rope and rubbed him on the head.

"This one's about broke, Mr. Ben."

"Good. We needed some good news." He laughed, and the crew joined in. "Only thirty-eight more to break."

The day passed with some of the horses turning into hoof-flashing tornados; others showed they were at least rope broken. Bruised, tired, and weary, his boys looked up as Digger came by riding his drag, reining his mules, and Billy Jim on the mare behind him.

"Whoa!" Digger shouted, hauling in the reins, and the mules stopped. Everyone nodded in approval. He clicked to them and they moved forward; then he swung them sideways to make them put their noses against the corral.

"You got them trained just in time to help us ride these escapees from hell," Chip said, and they all went to wash up.

Hap was ringing the dinner bell like a new Christmas present. Ben felt better about the horse deal than he knew he should. They were a long way from broken horses, but maybe they'd get enough edge off them for the boys to ride them. Days under the saddle on the trail would do the rest.

Martinez and the cattle were next — half a herd to bring home. In the morning he'd take the wagon to town and get the supplies Hap would need for the drive down there and back. He'd find Digger some clothes, too.

Washing up outside the house in the pans set out by Hap, the crew talked about the new horses and the names they chose, like Screw-tail, Shotgun, Socks, Big Bob, Sleepy, Damn Near Broke, Kangaroo, Darter, and so on. Lathering hands and forearms, then faces, then rinsing themselves, and they dried on the towels hung over the pegs and sauntered inside, bringing the cook up to speed on what happened that day.

"I'm going to town in the morning," Ben announced. "I'll mail letters and buy tobacco, and I'll even kiss any pretty young lady that's missing any one of you."

His words drew smiles from the crew. He heard no requests and wiped the corner of his mouth, then headed for the line filling their tin plates with food.

"Mr. Ben, you can kiss a pretty one and tell her you did it for me," Billy Jim said from behind him in the line.

"Oh, no, I want to kiss your girlfriend, not find you one." He turned and noticed he'd embarrassed the youth.

"Maybe you'll find one in Mexico," Mark offered.

"Plenty pretty ones down there," Chip assured him, turning back from topping his full plate with two soda biscuits.

"I don't speak enough Spanish to get her name," Billy Jim said.

"Aw, love don't take no language," Chip assured him. "It simply happens."

Ben could swear to that. He'd talked less to Jenny than to any woman in his life. In east Texas, he recalled at Billy Jim's age courting Myra Cole. They danced on Saturday night and during breaks they walked in the woods holding hands and kissing. Then, heavyhearted after the dance, they parted each time, and she went home in the family wagon for church on Sunday — Lutheran church. He was Baptist, when he went. Her folks didn't approve of her paying attention to such a boy who didn't go to Mass.

Then she told him her father had told her she must marry a man ten years older. A man with four small children whose wife had died of a burst appendix. Tears streamed down her smooth face when she told Ben there was nothing he could do, and she ran off after telling him not to follow her.

He saw her months later in town, her belly swollen with her first pregnancy. She smiled at him when he removed his hat and blocked her way. Her eyes mirrored how tired she was.

"Ben McCollough, how nice you look."

"So do you," he said quickly, feeling an unseen hand at his Adam's apple threatening to choke off his air. Damn, four kids to tend and her own bogging her down. He fought back the tears that threatened.

"God be with you," he said, and hurried on, lest he shot her unthinking husband or did something worse. Up on the Brazos, three months later, the news came to him that she had died in childbirth. The whole thing was like the wind in the cottonwoods; it swept over him and was gone. At least he wouldn't have to worry about her anymore.

Beth Day, a young widow, stole his heart about the time the war started. He was torn between his obligations to Texas and to her. But she needed someone to run her ranch, not someone to run off to fight a war over succession, states' rights, and slavery.

"You don't even own a slave," she said, shaking her head in disgust. "You ride out of here, Ben McCollough, I swear it's over between us."

He finished cinching his horse and nodded that he'd heard her. If she could forget him that easily, he guessed the missing him wouldn't last very long. He mounted his horse, tipped his hat, and headed for Austin to sign up for the army.

After that he took up with painted ladies and doves. The last time he was serious was with Millescent Burns in Teeville. She never was serious about him, and he decided his one-sided attraction was finally over one day and rode out of town, convinced that he would never have a wife. He'd sure wasted a lot of time on Millescent.

At Hailey Hanager's funeral, someone during the supper on the church grounds introduced him to Mrs. Jenny Fulton. She wiped an errant wave of honey-brown hair back, curtsied, and nodded politely.

"I guess your man's running cows too," Ben said, not thinking that anyone that beautiful might not be married.

"He was killed in the war," she said, and lowered her gaze.

"You and these boys —"

"We have a few cows and calves." Her eyes met his, and he saw the determination in them.

"I can ever help, you send word. I'm sorry — I never knew about any widows in the country." He shook his head.

"Thanks, Mr. McCollough."

"Ben, Mrs. Fulton."

"Jenny, Ben."

"Yes, ma'am, Jenny."

So periodically he sent Hap over with a fat deer he shot and dressed for her. The best thing he ever did was hire Mark to help at the past spring's roundup. The youth made a good hand, and Ben knew he deserved to go up to Kansas if his mother could spare him.

"Mr. Ben, mail this please, sir."

Ben looked up and took the envelope from Chip. "Be glad to."

He watched the older hand walk out the door into the twilight. He wondered who Sonja Van Dam was at a San Antonio address. No telling. Chip could be writing anyone — a love, a dove, a cousin; he'd probably never tell, either. Ben shook his head. He'd better get a bath and clean up before he went to bed. He'd hate to show up in town like some dodger riding the chuckline.

Ready for bed, he tossed some wood on the fireplace coals. The room had the chill of fall inside. Where was Hap? He usually had it warm enough in there to cook a fellow. He turned an ear. Someone was singing and playing a guitar — it must be Miguel. He went to the open door and bent over to listen to the music.

The boy could sing those Spanish ballads. He shook his head and yawned. Working this crew was harder than doing things himself. He'd best go get the hot water in the tin tub and bathe; maybe he could stay awake that long. *Kansas, Kansas, I'm coming. Fast as I can, Jenny.*

Chapter 7

Ben stuck his Spencer in the wagon box and climbed up. The two bays were dual-purpose animals: They were stout enough to haul the wagon and could be used as saddle ponies on roundup. Mark held them by the bridles and waited for his signal to release them. Ben, standing in front of the spring seat, searched around for his crew.

"Take your time breaking them to tie and lead. Chip can ride any that act broke, but everyone be careful; they're still full of piss and vinegar."

They waved that they'd heard him, but he knew they wouldn't listen. The competition was about to begin for the bronc-buster title. It would be high, wide, and handsome. Why, at that age he'd much rather have ridden a good bucking horse than a Ferris wheel he'd once seen in San Antonio. If only he were a small mouse in one of those boys' vest pockets for that day. Things would get rowdy. He clucked to make the bays trot — he wanted to be back before dark.

He passed the Logan place and was winding up through the cedars to get up on the mesa when a shot splintered the top of the sideboards behind the spring seat. If the shooter had been a little better, Ben knew he'd been pushing up daisies.

In response he shouted at the bays and went to throwing them the reins. He needed out of this brushy mess before the bushwhacker took another potshot at him. At the top of the ridge he'd have this back-shooter out in the open, if he wanted to go after him.

The cedar's boughs rushed by. The ruts and rocks threw Ben from side to side, but he managed to stay on the spring seat. Another shot cracked above the clatter of wagon, charging horses, and harness. At last they crested the flat top. Then he hurried eastward, shouting at them to run, glancing over his shoulder for any sign of pursuit. Rain Crow had told him to watch out for Coulter. Was the angry drunk after him? Someone wanted him dead. He had good evidence in the splintered sideboard. He drew up, used his foot on the brake handle, and reined the horses down to a walk.

The Spencer close by, he was ready in this open brown grassland for a fight. He bet the coward wouldn't come out. He let the horses stand and catch their breath. With the brake set and the reins tied off, he searched the western horizon. No shooter. That was all right. His time would come.

In Teeville he stopped off at the lawman's house and reported the shooting to deputy Robert Kilmer. Kilmer had heard that Harold Coulter was putting out talk about "getting" Ben.

"Well, he must have tried today," Ben said.

"I see the hole. He got close," Kilmer said, looking at the damaged sideboard. "I'll watch for him."

"Thanks," Ben said; then he drove over to the store. Hap's list included two hundred pounds of flour, two big cans of baking powder, twenty pounds of sugar, two gallons of molasses, two hundred pounds of dry frijoles and a hundred pounds of rice, a gallon of vinegar, a case of canned tomatoes, and one of peaches, two lard tubs, some sides of fatback, raisins, and dried apples. If he saw anything else he wanted to eat he would be sure to throw it in too.

Mrs. Whitaker was busy sending the hired boys after things to fill his list.

"You get that material sewed up?" she asked.

"What?" he asked, not understanding the question.

"The bolt of material you bought a few days ago."

"Oh, that bolt. No, not yet." He wanted to tell her to start extending his credit to Jenny, but then she'd surely figure out who had received the material. He was damned if he did or didn't.

"Oh, ma'am, Mrs. Fulton and her sons are going to be taking care of my place while we're gone, so if she needs anything put it on my bill."

"Nice of you. I'm sure she can use the income, but I hardly can see how a woman and two young boys can do much for a farm."

"They'll do fine," he said, holding back his temper. "Better than some of these drifters in the country, anyway."

"It's your farm."

"Ranch," Ben said to correct her. He wasn't a farmer. He grew cattle, not cotton.

"As you say, Mr. McCollough."

"Ben," he said.

"Yes, Ben. Is this cash or credit?"

"Cash," he said, still not certain whether he would use Whitaker's credit for his supplies. A busybody like Whitaker's wife had about made him lose his temper. She'd be talking about Jenny, too, before he got out of town. Why couldn't folks leave things alone that weren't any business of theirs? He would never know, and stormed out, forgetting to thank the boys who worked there and loaded the wagon.

Then a cold chill ran up his spine. Was someone out there somewhere waiting to dry-gulch him. He'd better get his wits about him. He reached down, straightened the Spencer, then headed his team for the ranch, the sun already showing past two o'clock. It would be after dark before he got back home, at this rate. *Jenny, Jenny, I won't see you until we get back from Mexico.*

Chapter 8

Ben's hands found a good use for prickly pear cactus — target practice. His armed men took shots from their horses as they rode by the patches. He had plenty of black powder and lead. The riders were shooting at the pads and some dried-up fruit. They were doing better, and several pears had .30- and .44-caliber holes shot in them.

The betting was going on, and several months' pay looked to be at stake. Chip missed a few, and Billy Jim moved to the fore as money winner. His keen squint and determination were winning over suave Chip's cockiness.

"Where did you learn to shoot like that?" Mark asked Billy Jim.

"I guess my paw. He can put six shots in a pie pan."

"Not riding by," Chip said.

"Yeah, he was a shell shucker during the war," Billy Jim said. "They taught him how to shoot — Quantrill did."

"Your father was with him?"

"Sure, he knew Frank and Jessie and them Youngers."

"Wonder them carpetbaggers ain't rounded your paw up." Chip shook his head in disbelief.

Billy Jim nodded his head at him. The cap-and-ball Colt reloaded; he sent five more lead balls through the next pear pad sticking up.

"Why ain't you shooting, Digger?" Ben asked.

"I's going to, Mr. Ben. But I been listening to all these here gun experts so I be ready."

"Fire away, Digger; they ain't experts," Ben said, and shared a wink with his black cowboy, realizing he'd forgotten all about getting Digger's new clothing. Maybe in Mexico he'd find him an outfit.

Ben caught up with Hap and the wagon. He could hear more shots and smiled. Digger would be all right with the pistol.

"When they going to run out of ammo?" Hap shouted over the jingle of harness, the sound of hoofbeats, and ringing of the iron rims on the hard ground.

"Couple of days," Ben said, taking off his hat and wiping the sweat off his forehead with his sleeve. The sun turned up warmer than it had been in a week. They were in

110

mesquite country: gnarled ancient mesquite, many dead, some greasewood, sprawling beds of prickly pear cactus, and long dried grass.

"When you gonna wear that new shirt she made you?"

"When we start north."

"Saving it?"

"Yeah," Ben said absently. "For good luck."

"Who's this shooter made that hole in my rig?"

"Rain Crow says his name's Harold Coulter. Robert Kilmer said he had some brothers and they all were troublemakers."

"Why's he mad at you?"

"Damned if I know. I think he was drunker than a hooter and stood up to me when I started to leave this joint. I just threw him aside. Guess he landed wrong."

Hap chuckled. "I seen you throw folks aside before. Here," he shouted to one of his horses for doing something wrong. "It ain't the easiest way to land."

"I figure a man won't face you with a gun, then he's afraid, and scared folks are the worst kind you can deal with."

"I agree. Where we camping tonight?"

"A small ranch up ahead. Santos Montoya's."

"I know now. I don't make this run with you to the border often enough to remember all the stopovers."

Ben twisted in the saddle. His riders were coming. They'd left without Dru Nelson, but maybe when he showed he'd find the note Ben had left tacked on the door for him. The man might have had some trouble.

Santos Montoya greeted them in late afternoon when they drove up to his jacal-and-brush corrals. His beard was gray and his face lined from many days in the sun. He nodded to the riders and welcomed them. An ample-bodied woman rushed out and hugged Ben when he dismounted.

"Ah, Silva," Ben said, holding her out to look at her. "You are as pretty as ever."

"Such a liar you are, Ben McCollough." Then she threw her head back and laughed freely. "Ah, these young men ride with you this time."

"My vaqueros."

"I will kill a fat goat to feed them," she said, hands on her hips and the low-cut blouse exposing her coffee-colored cleavage.

"My *compadre* Hap has beans and rice."

"Oh, he is your cook." She threw her head back to appraise Hap.

"Yes, ma'am, and as soon as I get these horses out of harness I'll be right along to help on the goat-butchering business." Hap started off the wagon.

"Better yet, the boys can handle the horses," Ben said, and gave a head toss to his men. They smiled and agreed, dismounting and undoing their own cinches.

"She got any hot water?" Ben asked Santos.

"Sure."

"Bet you're ready as I am for a fresh cup of coffee."

"Oh, my, *sí*. We have been out for a while. When I get time I will go buy some."

He was probably out of *dinero* to buy some, too. Ben climbed up in the wagon to get some and returned with a sack of roasted fresh-ground coffee. He followed Santos inside while the boys unhitched the team.

"So many cowboys?"

Ben poured the coffee in the boiling pot and straightened. "I've got some steers bought in Agua Fría. About half as many as I need."

"Be careful there, *señor*. Many bandits are on the border these days. Not like the old days."

"I don't know much about it. I've contracted some cattle before down there from

Benito Martinez. We were on a deal for eight hundred head. But he only has four hundred."

"Why only four hundred?"

"To be honest, I think all this talk about cattle drives has him thinking others will pay more for them."

Santos pinched his beard. "You may be right, *señor.*"

"You hear anything about cattle sales?"

"Only what my cousin he says; they are only paying them fifty centavos for big steers that they round up."

"Was he having trouble getting big steers?"

"Always trouble with the big ones. They live in the brush and are like deer: They only come out to graze at night. But Mother of God, there are more cattle in the brush on both sides of the Rio Bravo than ten thousand men could gather."

"I'll keep my eyes and ears open down there." Ben could hear Silva and Hap talking nonstop as she came in holding up by the hind leg the young goat carcass they'd already skinned.

After supper, the boys spread their bedrolls out near the wagon. Ben squatted on his boot heels to talk to them.

"Santos says the bandits are bad down at

the border. So I want you boys to stay together. They might try to rob us. Miguel, you know much more?"

"There are some bad *hombres* there."

"Will you listen for anything and be sure we don't get double-crossed? Times before there have been men bought cattle on the border and they were robbed and the cattle stolen back."

"Oh, *sí*. I know some people down there who would tell me anything they know."

"From here on ride with your eyes and ears open. And your six-guns close by. 'Night."

" 'Night, Mr. Ben," came the chorus.

Two days later, Ben could see the pale green cottonwood tops in the distance. The Rio Bravo, which most Texans called the Rio Grande, lay about an hour ahead. Harness chains jingled and the horses' trotting made a drumbeat on the sandy ground. Agua Fría sat upon the escarpment across the watery border. And the usual washerwomen would be scrubbing their clothes and give his boys an eyeful of bare brown breasts when they rode past.

"Digger," Ben called out, and the black hand spurred his horse to catch up.

"Yes, sah?"

"The crew wants you to look like a cowboy. I'm going over there and look for my cattle buyer. You want to ride along, I'd advance you enough money to buy some duds."

Mischief danced in the deep brown pools of his eyes and he glanced down at his faded one-piece outfit. "They don't like my overalls?"

"I guess they'd like you to dress . . . well, like they do."

"I'd sure be proud to do that. What you think it's going to cost?"

"Hat, pants, shirt, vest or serape, some footgear and a sombrero — hmm. Five, six dollars."

"Gots to have a bandanna."

"Oh, yes."

"I'm ready."

"I'll be so in a few minutes," Ben said, and nodded. He rode back to the others. "I'm advancing five a man. Be here and ready to herd cattle at daybreak. Don't lose any of my horses or saddles, since most of them are mine and it would be a long drive to Kansas riding bareback."

"I'll have supper here at six," Hap said, looking over the crew whom Ben had paid. They began shaking their heads — no, they'd miss it.

"Good, I won't cook no supper," Hap said, and scratched the beard stubble on his cheek. "I may go see the city lights then too."

"Same goes for you. If I can get Martinez going we'll have cattle to herd at daybreak."

"We'll be here, Captain."

"Good. Let's go, Digger." Ben mounted his roan. "If we all leave they might rob the camp."

"I'll stay," Billy Jim offered.

"Be careful then," Ben said, wondering if he'd left any guard at all.

"Naw. I ain't got no business over there," Hap said. "Billy Jim, you go along, keep them boys out of trouble."

"Thanks," Ben said, feeling better about Hap's decision. "You ready, Digger?"

"Yes, sahree, I be ready," Digger said, and swung up into the saddle in a bound.

Ben couldn't put his finger on anything, but the itching up his spine made him look about more than usual. During time spent in the war, he recalled the same feelings. He and Digger bailed their horses into the Rio Grande and splashed across the knee-deep stream. The washerwomen talked to them in Spanish, and Digger grinned as if pleased to be with him for their frontal show.

"Mr. Ben, how's you know a bandit from the rest of 'em?"

"That's the hard part," Ben said.

"Well, I just wondered. I'm looking a lot, but I ain't sure I'd knows one."

"Take my word, you will."

"Kinda like a dog runs out barking, huh — you knows real quick if'n he's just barking or gonna bite you."

Ben laughed and agreed.

They found Digger a pair of striped pants and a collarless cotton shirt. Two women waited on them in the shop, and they soon brought him a selection of serapes. Digger took a gray one, then a high-crowned straw hat.

His word for *bandanna* and their Spanish one was not translating until he pointed to Ben's. Then they both nodded, and one ran off while the other showed him boots. He made faces trying them on.

Ben found a pair of soft leather boots and tossed them to Digger.

"Naw, them don't hurt my feet," he said, stomping around in them.

The women smiled in relief and so did Digger as he walked around in his new footgear. "How much *dinero?*" he asked.

One girl began to count using her fingers and mumbling numbers. "Ten pesos."

"Oh, no," Digger said. "Three."

"Ten!" she shouted.

The bickering went on; the manager came over, and they went over the items.

Ben squatted on his boot heels, amused over the haggling. Digger needed no lessons in border dickering. He could get right in and argue with the best. In the end, Ben paid the man four dollars and six bits. Outside he gave Digger his five dollars and sent him off to find the rest of the boys.

Ben rode his horse to the livery, left the roan there — too easy to steal him off the hitch rail — and walked two blocks to look for Martinez in the La Paloma Cantina.

"Ah, *mi amigo* Ben," the cattle buyer said at the sight of him.

Ben looked over the crowd in the dimly lit place. Hard to see much of anything except near the small candle lights on the tables.

"You want a drink?" Martinez asked

"Beer," Ben said, and took a place, nodding to the heavy-jowled other man seated at the table with him.

"*Señor* Salano, I want you to meet my friend from Texas, Ben McCollough."

"Glad to meet you, *señor*." The man never offered his hand, so Ben let him go. He listened as Martinez arranged to get beer with the barmaid.

"Ah, I have the steers," Martinez said,

and slid in beside Ben. "You wish to go look at them?"

"How many?" He could see them at delivery — how many and the price was the thing at the moment for Ben.

"Four — four-fifty." Martinez shrugged.

"When do I get the rest you promised me?"

"Oh, it is hard to get that many big steers." Martinez shook his head as if troubled.

Ben tapped his index finger on the table. "Martinez, I can get them bought. You either get me the rest of them or I'll look elsewhere."

"Ah, *Señor* Ben — I will do my best."

"Best ain't good enough. I want the rest of the steers."

"These cattle, they cost more." Martinez squirmed in his seat. Salano looked as if he had nothing to do with the matter.

The girl delivered his beer and Ben sat back to sip it. He wiped his mouth on the back of his hand. "Two dollars is all I am paying across the river for big steers."

"They cost —"

Ben shook his head. "Fifty cents a head is all you pay those brush poppers for their delivery."

Like a banty rooster, Martinez rose up,

showing his indignation. "Oh, but I have more expenses."

Ben waved his complaint away. "So do I."

"You are ready for the delivery?"

"Yes, put them across the river in the morning."

"Two-fifty?"

"We had a deal last fall for two dollars, and you better find the rest of them."

"Pay me two-fifty."

"And the rest of them?"

"I will have to find them. You can pay me?"

"Yes. If you'll bring four hundred big steers I'll pay you two-fifty." He grew weary of Martinez, the place, and his company, the shifty-eyed one he called Salano. Something was not right — Ben didn't have his finger on the problem, but he'd been in enough fixes during the war to trust his senses. Maybe it was all the Spanish being spoken. He knew enough to be conversational, but something was amiss in the smoky atmosphere of the cantina.

"You pay me two-fifty?"

"I will if they're big steers — no trash, no heifers, and no old mossy horned ones either. That's prime price."

Martinez agreed, and Ben stood up. The deal was made. If only he could have gotten all the cattle at one time he'd have felt better.

The skin on the back of his neck crawled as he walked the block back to the livery after he left the cantina. He'd better have the boys ready for anything, to back him if necessary. The youth brought the roan out and he paid him ten centavos, checked the cinch with his back to the wall so he had a good view of the narrow street in both directions, and once in the saddle headed for the red-light district.

He found the newly dressed Digger standing guard over the boys' horses on a vacant lot. A broad smile on his ebony face, he wore a sombrero on his shoulders.

"Mr. Ben?"

Ben leaned over and lowered his voice. "Tell the boys I think we have some problems. Might be better if they all eat supper at the camp."

Ben straightened in the saddle, checked around, and saw little activity in the late afternoon: a few sleepy cur dogs panting in the shade, a woman or two wearing colorful head coverings, going shopping perhaps. Still, he felt on edge.

"Maybe Miguel can learn something in town about a double cross." Ben checked the impatient roan. "But tell him to take no chances."

"We be there; yous tell that old Hap we's coming for supper. Make him moan, won't it?" Digger laughed out loud. "Him's got his feet up and resting."

"I'd rather hear him moan than someone get hurt. Take care," Ben said, then swung the roan around and headed for the river.

"You've got nothing to go on but a gut feeling?" Hap asked as he shoveled coals on the Dutch oven lid, then set it on a small pile of red-hot chunks from his fire.

"Nothing, but I know Martinez is up to something. This buddy of his, Salano, is some fish-eyed guy. Martinez talks business in front of him like they're partners."

"Why deliver only half the steers now?"

"Maybe to size us up," Ben said. "I mean, if they think they could get the money and steal back the steers they could sell them to someone else and play the same trick on them."

"Hard to tell bandits from the good guys down here." Hap looked off toward the river. "Kinda wish we had them Spencers you're buying."

"It would be nice." Using a kerchief from his back pocket for a pot holder, Ben poured himself a fresh cup of coffee. He gazed over at the jackals on the hillside bathed in the

123

blood-red of sundown.

"They coming back?"

"They'll be here. Maybe a little drunk on cactus juice and worn out from their attempts to conquer and subdue the entire *puta* population. But they'll be coming."

He looked again toward the sounds coming from Mexico and smiled. Those whooping-it-up riders hitting the river abreast were his drovers. *Thank God.*

"Going to be hard, Ben," Hap said.

"How's that?" Ben asked, looking through the vapors off his too-hot-to-drink cup.

"Having to listen to all that bravado about what lovers they are." Hap chuckled and stirred the bean kettle with a long wooden spoon. "Glad I ain't that young all over again." He put both hands on his hips and straightened. "Why, it makes my back ache to think about it."

Ben nodded that he heard him. The boys were all back — no, he could see Miguel was missing. He hoped that boy was careful. No way they'd play nice, if what he suspected really existed. He kicked a pile of dry horse apples asunder — no one said his plans for this Kansas drive would all be smooth.

Chapter 9

"Not going to be much moon tonight," Chip said, squatting down beside Ben.

"Maybe why they wanted to put off selling me these steers until now," Ben said, watching the pearly starlight on the rippled surface of the Rio Grande.

"Could be. I heard the cattle earlier."

"They have some over there. Better be big steers or I'm not taking them."

"What's keeping Miguel?" Mark asked.

Ben shook his head. He set the Spencer aside and leaned it against the small mesquite tree. They had a good view of the river from their vantage point despite the lack of moonlight. Perhaps all his concerns about bandits were unfounded; still, it never paid to take chances.

The sound of the water rushing by, night insects buzzing, and a few lonely coyotes howling made the night's orchestration. Once in a while some loud voices carried over from the village, but nothing much.

"I spent lots of nights like this with the

rangers," Chip said. "Course, I was sweating some Comanches sneaking up and whacking me over the head. You can get so uptight you want to scream too."

"Like war, it's hell," Ben said.

"Rider coming."

Ben agreed, making out the outline. Maybe it was Miguel; he hoped so.

He straightened and swept up the rifle. "I'll go see what he knows."

"*Señor* McCollough?" the voice asked.

Definitely not Miguel's voice. Ben shifted the rifle in his hands and cocked the hammer. "*Sí.*"

"Some *banditos,* they are holding Miguel, *señor.*"

"How did you know me?"

"I am Miguel's cousin, Toledo. He was talking to a *puta* named Mia and these two *banditos* jumped him. They took him to a cathouse."

Was this a trap? Ben would have to chance it. Miguel was working for him. "Who are the *banditos?* You know their names?"

"No, but they are bad *hombres.* They work for Salano."

"Who's he?" Ben asked, hoping for an answer to his own question about the man.

The youth shook his head. "He owns

126

some cantinas and a cathouse."

"Does he have many bad *hombres* work for him?"

"*Sí*, some bad ones."

"This place where they have him, can we get Miguel out alive?"

"Oh, I hope so."

"Chip, get three horses. I'll wake up the boys. We better get going." He turned to Toledo. "Can you use a gun?"

He held out his hands. "I can use one, but I don't have one."

"I'll load you one. Don't shoot me or my men is all I ask."

"*Sí, Señor* McCollough."

He already was covering the sandy ground to the bedrolls. "Everyone up; we've got big problems."

"Huh?"

"Hap, you, Digger, and Billy Jim need to guard the camp. Salano's men have taken Miguel prisoner."

"Taken Miguel? What we going to do?" Hap asked, jerking on his pants.

"Mark, Chip, Toledo, and I are going over there and get him out."

"It could be a trap." Hap jerked his belt tight.

"Could be. You watch things. We don't come back, you boys may as well go home.

127

Loan me your pistol," Ben said to Hap.

He handed it over to him. "Like hell we're leaving you or them here —"

"Hap, if the four of us can't handle it, an army can't."

"Damn it, Ben, be careful."

He nodded with the extra pistol in his waistband and hauled his saddle to the outline of the horses that Chip had returned with. The blanket in place, he threw on the saddle and reached under for the cinch. His mind ran through a thousand things.

"Here, Toledo." Handing him the handgun, he said, "Boys, we don't need to shoot each other. We need to be ready, but use a split second's worth of caution too."

"Yes, sir."

They mounted up and crossed the river. Toledo led the way; he swung them around the village so they came in from the south. Ben thought he could see the bedded-down cattle on a starlit flat. They rode up a steep trail to the back of some houses, dismounted, and hitched their reins to some mesquite brush.

Toledo pointed to the crest and a sprawling building with several lights in scattered windows. Ben considered a plan. If he and Toledo went into the place, secured one of the working girls, and got her to lead them to Miguel, maybe they could get in and out with little bloodshed or shooting.

"Chip, you and Mark stay here. If we can get to him, we may be coming on the run. Be ready to ride."

"Yes, sir. You need us, we'll sure come help."

"I understand, but we take too many up there, it might wake up some sleeping giant."

"I savvy that," Chip said.

"We'll be here, Ben, if you need us," Mark said.

Ben acknowledged that he'd heard him and started after Toledo.

"You know this place?" he asked with his Colt in his hand.

"Some. I been here a few times."

"Good."

They entered through the back way. The youth led the way. Toledo pointed to a shadow and both drew back. Ben could smell the strong musk of females — perfume and powder. That mixed with stale cigar smoke, whiskey, men's sweat, and body odors saturated the air in the dark side hallway.

Mumbling and singing to himself, a tall man came down a well-lit hall and turned in to the dark one where they stood against the wall. Ben bounced a gun barrel over his head and he collapsed. With the unconscious man rolled over, Ben ripped the handgun from his holster.

"One of Salano's men," Toledo whispered.

"Good, we've got one less. Do we have to check all these rooms for him?" He jammed the man's handgun behind his belt buckle.

"I don't know which one he could be in."

"Someone does. They know where he's at."

Toledo nodded, then looked down the hall and waved for Ben to follow him. Their way dimly lit by small, smoky candles at intervals, they hurried down the tile floor in the narrow confines. They stopped and listened at some loud hacking. A tough-talking guy in one of the rooms was coughing and ordered someone to get him some tequila — *muy pronto.*

A door began to open, and both of them froze against the wall. Unsuspecting, a woman closed the door with her back to them. Toledo reached out, clamped his hand over her mouth and jerked the wide-eyed, scantily clad girl to him.

"Where are they holding Miguel?" Ben hissed his best Spanish in her ear.

She shook her head.

"Damn it, where does Salano take his prisoners?"

This time she indicated down the hallway. Ben motioned for Toledo to take her that way.

"Don't scream or we'll kill you," Toledo said, and she agreed to his terms. Free of his hand over her mouth, she breathed heavily. She was hardly more than a teenager, but he hurriedly pushed her on. Ben kept their backs covered until she indicated two doors. Ben swung her and the youth back out of the way, filled his fists with both pistols, and used his boot heel to crash open the double door.

A *puta* screamed. In the dim light, a tall *hombre* went for his gun — too late. Ben snapped off a shot and sent him flying backward. Acrid gunsmoke boiled in the room and the candles went out. Someone crashed out the side window, and Ben tried to recall where he had last caught sight of Miguel, bound up in a chair.

He holstered his gun and took the skinning knife from behind his back. "See where they went. I'll get Miguel."

"They're getting away." And Toledo began firing his pistol out the window. Miguel was limp and cold when Ben touched the back of his hand to his face. He slashed the ropes binding him, put his knife away, bent over, and slung the boy's body over his shoulder.

"Let's get the hell out of here," he said to the youth standing by the starlit window.

"Good idea." Toledo raced over to the doorway. At the report of a pistol shot in the hallway, he jerked back.

"Out the window," Ben said. "We've got hornets stirred up in here." He ducked low to clear the unconscious Miguel through the casing, then stepped out onto the ground. A couple of doves were screaming at the top of their lungs. They may have been before, too, but Ben had been too busy to notice it.

Toledo fired a few more shots at the building to cover their retreat. No one returned fire. Chip and Mark came leading the horses with their guns drawn.

"Ben, what's happening?"

"Mount up. We've got Miguel."

"He okay?"

"Can't tell. He's out right now."

"What did they do to him?"

"He'll have to tell us."

"Were the girls in there pretty?" Mark asked, backing up at Ben's elbow with his gun drawn.

"About the same as the rest," Ben said,

putting the boy's body over the saddle. Mark helped him load Miguel and held the horse. Then Ben stepped up into the saddle to hold him over his lap.

"Let's get out of here."

When they splashed across the Rio Grande, Ben's back stopped itching. He felt relieved to see his three-man crew rush forward.

"What happened?" Hap asked as Chip and Mark eased Miguel down.

"They're going to double-cross us, *Señor* Ben. They are going to deliver the steers, then stampede them back across the river," Miguel managed in a weak voice, when they lowered him onto a blanket.

"I thought so," Ben said. He knelt beside the pale-faced youth while someone held up the lantern from the wagon so he could see. "Any wounds?"

"No, but my head's sore where they beat on it," Miguel replied.

"Lay there; you'll get to feeling better."

"I am so glad to be out of that place. Whew."

"Who all was there?" Ben asked.

"Some guy named Salano — I don't know the others."

"What now, Ben?" Hap asked.

"I'm thinking of a way to welcome them."

"You mean you'd do business with those crooks and murderers?" Hap gave him a disapproving scowl.

"If I can get the cattle I need and get out of here, I don't give a damn if they're sissies."

The boys chuckled.

"Hap, you and two of the boys take your shotgun and my rifle; ride upstream. I figure the rustlers'll be coming across before daylight. If they're sending anyone over to stampede our cattle, they'll cross up there, because they need to get around us to stampede the cattle back across the river. Downstream is too open for them not to be seen."

"What'll you do?"

"When they bring them across, I'll look over the steers, count 'em, and buy 'em if they fit."

"But what if —"

"If you three can stop them so they can't stampede them back into the river, the rest of us may stampede them toward home."

Hap nodded in the candle's reflected light. "What about Miguel?"

"I'll be fine," the youth said in a hoarse voice.

"In the wagon you'll be safe," Ben said. "Toledo, you want to go to Kansas?"

"Ah, *sí, señor.*" A smile spread over his

134

dark face in the firelight.

"You're hired. Get Miguel comfortable in that wagon and fix him up with a loaded gun. Billy Jim, gather the horses and tie them on a picket line. I don't want them run off in the confusion. Then get back here; we'll need you and every gun we got."

"Yes, sir." And he ran off to obey.

"I's help him," Digger said, and headed off into the night.

"I'm taking Mark and Chip with me," Hap announced. "When we figure we've turned them back or they don't come, we'll come back and help you."

"Sounds good. Don't take any chances, boys. I need you healthy." That did not leave him with the most experienced hands, but he nodded. In minutes, two of the three were busy saddling horses, and Hap was digging out his brass twelve-gauge shells from a wooden ammo box in the wagon.

Billy Jim was standing close by when Ben poured himself a cup of coffee. "Guess this is some of that stuff you talked about?"

"It is. I didn't mean for it to happen so soon."

"Well, we signed on."

He smiled at the youth. "Bill, we're going to get those steers like he promised me, and we're going to Kansas, too. Going to be a cold day in hell before some two-bit border bandit outdoes you and me."

"I've been blowing holes in them cactus too," he bragged.

"I know you have. Guess Salano and his bunch should have been warned."

"They should have been."

"Better get a little shut-eye. I'll watch things and see about Miguel. We've got cattle coming in the morning."

" 'Night."

" 'Night, Mr. Ben," Digger said. "All them hosses be tied up close, like you say."

"Good, get a little sleep. Toledo, look in them pans if you haven't eaten. Hap usually has something left to gnaw on."

"*Sí.*" The youth went to rummage for something. "When will you go to Kansas?"

"When the grass greens in March. Until then I wanted to graze these cattle and settle them down, cut out the wildest ones. There's a blanket in the wagon to wrap up in; going to be cold around here in another hour." He tested the north wind by turning his face to its force — it had been trying to blow in all afternoon.

Blanket on his shoulders, he heard the distant pop of Hap's double-barrel scattergun. Double-shot buck from the muzzle of a Greener was a sure stopper at close range. Chip must be levering rounds from the Spencer, for the sounds of the shots were too smooth. So they had their heads down. Those bandits caught off guard in the faint light of the moon, crossing the river, could only hit the side of a barn if they were lucky.

Digger sat up in his blankets. "I better go see what's happening, Mr. Ben."

"Got your Colt loaded?" Ben asked.

"Oh, yes, sir."

"Digger, be careful; they may think you're one of the bandits."

"I be singing 'Yankee Doodle Dandy' when I gets close."

Ben chuckled. They ought to know no bandit could sing that song. "Go see."

After a half hour of his worrying, Ben heard horses and voices. He rose, shifted the Colt on his hip, and waited.

"Them bandits ain't coming back," Hap said when he rode in close and put his shotgun in the wagon by the seat. "When they was halfway across I stood up and told them in Spanish if they was rustlers, they better get their asses back to Mexico, and all hell broke loose. So I figured we had the right ones."

Ben agreed — he'd had lots of faith in his ex-noncom's expertise at leading a patrol.

Billy Jim was up by then, taking their horses and asking questions.

"I don't know, Bill, I ain't never killed a man before," Mark said, sounding troubled.

"Don't get no easier either," Chip said. "Won't ever get no easier."

Ben let the boys talk. Times like this, spilling your guts helped.

"How many?" he asked Hap.

"I think a dozen to fifteen. They came riding quiet. We let them get in the middle of the river before I challenged them. Then they opened fire. Caused the confusion I expected when we shot back. Hated about the horses getting shot, but we couldn't pick targets, only silhouettes."

Ben agreed and walked over to Mark. "Ain't nothing anyone can say. It's a tough deal. But I'd sure rather have him in the river floating for the gulf and you all unharmed."

"I understand, Ben," Mark said. "He wouldn't turn back. Kept coming. He could have reined his horse around. He was in the middle of the river — kept coming at me, shooting and screaming."

"You did what you had to do."

"I didn't think I could — I mean, shooting at them was one thing. But it came down to me and him."

Ben clapped him on the shoulder. "I'm sorry, but we've got more rivers to cross between here and there."

"I know. I won't wait the next time."

" 'Night, boys," Ben said, and went back to the wagon.

Hap handed him his whiskey bottle. Ben took a swig. The firewater cut all the way down to his stomach. It even cut the film off his teeth.

Your son did some growing up tonight, Jenny. That smart-mouthed ranger boy might make a real hand, and even Billy Jim would do. He shook his head at Hap's offer of another drink. Morning was only hours away.

Chapter 10

Dawn came like the soft glove of a woman sweeping the coating of dust off a deeply polished walnut gun stock. The sunshine's first light made the distant cottonwoods blurry in the glare. A cold wind out of the distant panhandle swept them. The fishy smell of the Rio Grande filled Ben's nostrils, and the bawling of cattle on the move in the distance made him feel better despite the fire holes he had for eyes that he tried to take all this in with.

Hap was busy feeding the boys. Digger and Billy Jim had all their day's horses on hand. It was time to herd cattle. Everyone had a case of the yawns, and Chip slapped his own face twice. "So I'm sure that I'm really here."

Martinez drove out in a one-horse buggy before the cattle ever came into sight. He reined up his mare and smiled as though nothing had ever happened.

"Good morning, *Señor* Ben."

"Morning, Martinez. All we've got is coffee."

"Oh, I've had mine. A drink, *señor?*" he asked, holding up some whiskey that looked golden in the direct sunbeams striking the bottle.

"No, Martinez, I have to be able to count, so you don't cheat me."

"Cheat you, *señor?* Why would I want to cheat you?"

"Last fall, you said, 'I will have eight hundred big steers on the border before Christmas.' Well, Christmas is only ten days away."

"I will find the others, but big steers —"

"How many you sending over?" Ben asked.

"Four hundred twenty — thirty."

"All big ones — three and four years old?"

"Most of them."

"You know how far it is to Abilene?"

"Where is this?" Martinez blinked his eyes.

"Kansas," Ben said, putting a boot on the buggy's iron step.

"No, I never been there."

"It's three months — four months up that way." He flung his arm northward.

"Long ways." Martinez squirmed in the seat.

"Long ways. They won't buy junk in Kansas. They won't pay for little *Mexican* calves."

141

Martinez set down the bottle and held up his hands. "In three weeks I will have the rest."

"Make it four weeks," Ben said.

"Why?"

"It will be full moonlight then and your bandit friends won't be able to sneak up on us."

"I have no bandit friends, *mi amigo*."

Ben shook his head. "That Salano is a big one."

"Oh, no, *señor*, he is my banker. No bandito — businessman."

"Miguel!"

The youth rode over.

"Take off your sombrero and show him what Salano's men did to you."

"Oh, I am so sorry. Must have been a big mistake."

"Boys, form a line on both sides. Billy Jim, you count them, Chip, you and Mark watch for limpers. Digger, you rope the ones they point out and drag them out."

Ben started to get in the saddle. He turned back. "You tell Salano I'll tack his hide to my outhouse next time he tries something on me."

"But . . . but —"

"I'll settle with you when we get the cattle counted and the culls cut out." Ben checked his horse. "How many more good ones have you got down there?" He gave a head toss toward Mexico.

"None, *señor.*"

"Better send your man back for the rest of the big ones. I seen lots of little steers in them coming out of the river."

An angry mask swept Martinez's face, and he drove his buggy to the river. Ben couldn't hear the trader's conversation with his *segundo,* but soon five of his men rode south in a hard gallop.

Ben surveyed the operation and his hands at work. Small steers were being shunted off to the side. Some were roped and dragged; others were cut out. Billy Jim stood in the stirrups as serious-looking as Ben had ever seen him, counting the passing cattle.

When the last of the dripping-wet cattle came up from the river and went past him, Billy Jim shouted, "Four hundred thirty."

"Good," Ben said, and rode over for a conference with Chip, Mark, and Digger, who sat their hard-breathing horses.

"How many small ones got by you two?"

"Not over a dozen head. Some slipped in and out and we had no time," Chip said, shaking his head.

"We cut back most of the limpers," Mark said.

143

"We got all we could, Mr. Ben," Digger said, wiping the sweat from his face on his sleeve.

Ben shook his head and held up his hand to dismiss their concern. "I'll pay him for a dozen small steers. How many did you boys cut?"

"I can count them," Mark said, and hurried off to make a survey.

The bunch of small and crippled steers, obviously hungry, were grazing hard, and Mark rode through them, making his census. He came back in a long trot.

"I counted twenty-seven head."

"Good, they're bringing some more; Billy Jim, count them," he warned his man at the approach of more steers across the river.

"They look okay?" Ben asked.

"They're walking all right," Billy Jim shouted. "Forty-two more."

Ben rode over to where Martinez sat in his buggy. He dismounted heavily, adjusted the holster, and dug out the sack of gold coins from his saddlebags.

Martinez climbed out of his rig and straightened his flat-brimmed black hat. "I'm sorry about the inconvenience, *señor*."

"I need four hundred more big steers." Ben met the man's gaze with a hard stare.

"When are you delivering them?"

"Ah *señor* —"

"Don't 'ah' me. I want the rest of your promise."

"In four weeks?"

"My boys counted twelve head of small steers in there that got by. I'm only paying a dollar a head for them. That means three hundred and ninety three in the first bunch, forty-two in the second one. That means I owe you ten thousand and ninety-seven dollars and change," Ben said, finished with his pencil calculations in his small logbook.

"That is all you counted?"

"There's twenty-seven culls over there."

"Twenty-seven!" Martinez slapped his forehead. "What would you give me for them?"

"Ten bucks."

"Ten dollars! Oh, Mother of God, how will I feed my little ones?"

"I ain't paying a dime more for that junk."

Martinez made a "give-me" sign with his fingers. Ben counted out eleven stacks of one hundred dollar bills. When he finished, Martinez swept them off the buggy seat where Ben had set them up in stacks, and gave Ben the difference owed.

"Four weeks, and they better be good steers."

"You don't understand, *señor*. There are no big steers left in the brush."

"Look harder," Ben said, and stepped into the saddle. He reined the roan around. "Tell that bandit Salano, next time we meet he better be packing a gun, too.

"Chip, you take the right lead, Mark the left. Miguel, you're on Chip's side. Toledo, you're on Mark's side. Digger, today you've got drag. Billy Jim, you help Hap get going and look after the horses. Later we'll swap positions.

"Let's head for home, boys."

"Yeah," came the roar, and they rode out to take their places.

Ben watched Martinez in his buggy head back for the river. Doing business with a liar was not his cup of tea — would the man have the rest of his cattle in four weeks? No way to know. He still had time before he started north. Blair told him uniform sets of large steers sold the best. But his plans depended on having at least an eight-hundred-head drive to top the market with. No knowing and damn sure no telling what they'd try next time, either.

He touched his spur to the roan. He needed to find a campground and a place to graze them later that day. Close to nine already he decided, checking the sun. The steers acted hungry to him — must not have been much graze over in Mexico where they held them.

"Get those culls. I bought them too," he shouted to Digger.

"We gets 'em, Mr. Ben." And Digger waved him on.

Chapter 11

By scouting ahead, Ben found a small creek to water the cattle. There was lots of dry grass and even some sprouting green through the bunches from the last rain. Should be lots of wild oats sprouting from the past rains, too, Ben decided. It would sure fatten his steers; they appeared to be pretty hollow, but most desert cattle out of Mexico looked that way. Mature steers on good forage fattened at an astounding rate. Small ones usually grew some more, but didn't fatten, which was his reason for buying the older ones. He wanted to walk them slowly to Abilene, have them slick as moles, and top that market. It wasn't a senseless drive he planned for them, so that when he arrived there they'd be fleshy. That would take longer, but in the end make him the most money. Heading those steers north in a trot would get them there in less than two months — but those lean greyhounds he arrived with wouldn't bring anything.

Satisfied with the creek campsite, he tied a red rag on a mesquite top about head high to mark it and headed back to tell Hap. What came next? The weeklong drive home. He wiped the grit out of the corners of his mouth with his thumb and thought about Jenny. Be a new way of life for him, to have a wife. He looked forward to it.

He short-loped the roan through the dead brush country. The black brush and tree skeletons cast a grim look to the rolling country. It would be good to get back to the live oaks and running water of home.

He rested the roan and waited for the approaching wagon. Billy Jim was bringing the horse herd after him. He hoped the boys were doing as well with the steers. The steers had been bunched for a while, and he could hope that they weren't too wild, but anything could happen to that many spooky cattle.

"Got camp picked. You and Billy Jim get the water you'll need before the cattle muddy it up. I hung a red flag in the brush for you as a marker."

"Good enough. We'll find it. You reckon them birds will try us again?" Hap asked.

"I won't bet against it," Ben said.

Hap stood in the wagon looking back for signs of the herd on their back trail. Ben thought he could see a trace of dust on the horizon.

"I'll check on them. You and Billy get camp set up. They'll be hungry as bears by the time they get here in midafternoon."

"You know it ain't far back to Mexico from here," Hap said.

Ben nodded that he heard him. Maybe eight or nine miles from the river was all they'd make that day. They still would be a tempting target for Salano and any other rustlers. In fact, Ben felt certain that until they were halfway home, nothing but a bullet in their head or heart would stop the bandits from trying to take the herd.

In early afternoon from a rise he surveyed the cattle coming in a long, serpentine train. He could see his men in place, stretched out for over a half mile, save poor Digger riding drag, and he was somewhere back in the dust that over sixteen hundred hooves churned up. They'd all get a chance at the job. Then if one of them was hurt, sick, or gone, someone else would know how to handle that job.

Ben rode in and joined Mark. "What do you think of longhorns now?"

"They want to go too fast at times, but Chip and I've backed off and they seem to slow some. I think they're hungry. We can fill them, they'll be easier to slow down. They're going too fast, aren't they?"

"Yeah, I'd like them to be more leisurely. They're damn near in a trot."

"I figured that," Mark said over the clatter of horns, hooves, and bawling cattle.

"Don't worry; we'll be in camp in an hour and they can eat all they want there."

"What about the water?"

"Near level-bank creek; they shouldn't pile in on each other."

"See you," Mark said, and Ben drifted back to find Toledo swinging a rope with a leather popper on the end.

"Going okay?"

"Ah, *sí, Señor* Ben, *gracias* for taking me along."

"You're welcome, though you may cuss me before Kansas for asking you on."

Toledo, his coffee-brown face floured with dust, laughed. "I am a vaquero, and we like to work."

"Good," Ben said, and dropped back, pulling up his kerchief to filter some of the dust. Out of nowhere, Digger burst in on his ring-eyed horse, both coated in the pale soil of south Texas.

"Boss man, you scared me. I thought you were a rustler."

"Sorry. How is the job going?"

"Besides the dust, it's not bad."

"Wind's coming up, and that should

151

help," Ben offered.

"Hope it comes soon. I better go check — I got some really poky ones."

"Be in camp in an hour," Ben promised and waved good-bye. He let the herd go on and the dust around him settle on the land. Sitting on a high point, he surveyed the country to the south. No sign of any dust from riders on the horizon — but he wouldn't sleep easy until they were back home at his ranch. In four weeks they'd come back and get the rest — he hoped.

After watching for any sign of pursuit for over twenty minutes, he fell in and rode north after the herd, satisfied. They'd be to camp by the time he got to the head of the line.

The hungry steers took quick drinks; then, bawling, they crossed the nearly dry creek and began harvesting bunches of grass on the next flat. Ben watched them, pleased for the most part. They didn't act too volatile. Mature steers were the worst. Most had been in the thorny thickets and not been touched since castration and branding as yearlings or even calves. The rest of their lives they'd successfully avoided humans.

Rainbow cattle, black, black-brown, red, and speckled, they came in all colors, he decided. A four- to six-foot span of horns on each head. Pushed close together on the move, the whack of horns sure made lots of noise, and in a thunderstorm green lightning danced across their heads. Ben hoped he never saw that happen again, but knew it was more than likely going north so early. They'd be there in time to dance with a tornado or two up on the plains.

"See anything out of place?" Hap asked when he rode into camp.

He gave his man a shake of the head and dropped out of the saddle. "No sign."

"Don't mean they ain't coming."

"Sure doesn't." Ben bent over, used the handkerchief from his pocket for a pot holder, and poured coffee in his tin cup. "For now we can rest."

"Got the boys coming in for coffee and fried pies in shifts," Hap said.

"You and Billy make them?"

"Naw, Bill did most of the work. I was laying out supper while he did that."

"Where's he at?"

"Out relieving cowboys — he missed getting in on the action today."

Ben nodded that he heard him. Billy Jim didn't want to be only the horse wrangler. The strong coffee revived Ben. Then he went to water his pony and turn him out for the night. It would be a half hour before sundown, but already the cattle were beginning to act full and drop down to chew their cuds. That should settle them in for the night.

They didn't need any wild stampede or rustlers spooking them. But it well could happen. *Be home in a week, Jenny. Love to see your face, not some dust-coated puncher's mug.* They'd be a long week getting there.

He closed his eyelids tight, wishing the tears he was forcing out would drive the gritty sand out from behind them. The tough work had begun.

After supper, Ben put Toledo and Chip on night herding for the first three hours. He had Billy Jim bring two horses he felt would be the easiest for them to use. Some horses never made night-herding animals. The good ones could slip around the herd with the cowboy on board talking or singing, never spooking or waking up animals in their circuit around the perimeter. They could see in the darkest night or the rainiest one, never stepped in a prairie dog hole nor lost their footing in a dead run to force the herd to circle back in a stampede. While none of his ponies had ever been on any drives except roundups, Ben had to think hard about the best to choose.

"Boys, sleep with your pistols. We're keeping horses saddled and on the picket line in case the *banditos* didn't get enough last night."

Everyone nodded, some went to bed, and the two night riders took off for the herd with Ben's instructions to sing or talk so that they didn't spook the bedded-down cattle.

He promised to wake up the next shift, Mark and Digger. Then he sat back and savored Hap's coffee. The Spencer close by, he listened to an owl hoot off in the growing darkness. He sure hoped those rustlers had enough from the night before, but one could never tell. After his coffee, he told Hap good-night and set out on his horse to see about things.

He stopped on a rise and turned his ear to the night wind for any sounds, but heard nothing save some insects and distant coyote yaps. Nothing — then an owl hooted and he saw the bird of prey riding the slight up drafts. His belly looked snow-white against the sky. Then he dove from the sky and a rabbit screamed in pain. The owl was fetching his supper. Ben booted his pony on westward, intending to make a wide circle, looking for any sign of trouble or a threat.

Nothing. He checked by the boys on

guard and they'd not heard or seen anything out of the ordinary. He went back to camp.

"All's well out there?" Hap asked in a sleepy voice.

"Not a thing."

"Good." The cook turned over, pulled the cover atop his head, and soon was lightly snoring.

Ben changed the guard. Mark and Digger rode out. That left Billy Jim and Miguel for the last one. Ben dozed a short while, then woke and walked out his stiffness in the cool air. He checked the Big Dipper. It would be another hour before the shifts changed.

His eyes felt like hot sand holes. The coffee left on the fire was too thick to stir and too bitter to drink. Two sips was too much, and he tossed it aside. He almost wished the bandits would come on so they could get it over with. *Damn.*

Two more sleepless nights and Ben felt they were over fifty miles from the border. The boys were settling into a routine and reading the Big Dipper for the time themselves. He threw his bedroll down before sunset that evening, crawled into it, and died.

That night he dreamed of the war, riding pell-mell through the Ozark roads, striking at the enemy in hit-and-run raids. Sympathizers hiding them. Women with hardly enough food for their own children killing precious chickens to feed them. Their own men off in Mississippi or Tennessee fighting for the same cause. No victories, only small efforts to thwart their opposition's efforts, shoot a few bushwhackers who took advantage of the helpless women to rob and steal.

One had been called Mike Robinson, a man taller than Ben. Robinson claimed he once broke a man's neck with his bare hands. He and his gang of thieves raided a farm. There were only three women there, a Mrs. Slater and two teenage daughters — the girls' father was off in the service of the Confederacy. Robinson took everything they had to eat, slapped around Mrs. Slater, then told his men to rape the girls. They rode off afterward, leaving the two girls senseless.

Ben's company of soldiers, led by some local operatives, found Robinson and his men half-drunk in a cave on the White River. They hanged them from an oak tree, shot them in the heart, and severed Robinson's head. His head in a gunnysack was delivered to the Union commander in Cassville, Missouri, with a note: *Your rapist. Cherish his head. Rebs.*

In a cold sweat, Ben woke up. The Colt in his hand, he sat there shivering and recalling Robinson's violent cursing when his men had dragged him out of the cave. The echoes had come out of the cavern long after they even had the madman outside. Hanging was too good for the likes of him. He had a vision of those poor girls, mumbling, cringing, crying out of their minds. Hanging had been too good a fate for him.

Chapter 12

The Christmas Eve dance at the Stallings Schoolhouse brought out everyone in the countryside. It had been a dull winter day that failed to really warm up. High cirrus clouds filtered out the sun's full heat, and Hap forecasted rain in two days. The steers acted settled enough in the country where they grazed them; he had left two boys to stay out there. Digger and Miguel had won the honors. Ben promised both of them extra time off for their sacrifice — Digger wanted to go to San Antonio before they started the drive north and see his mother; Miguel had some like plans, only Ben figured they were southward ones.

Ben took the buckboard he seldom drove over to pick Jenny up. Her boys all wanted to ride their own horses and had packed bedrolls to spend the night. Jenny needed to come home and milk her cow in the morning.

She wore her new dress made from the blue material and a nearly threadbare long gray coat that concerned Ben. How he could get her a new coat and not make her feel obligated, he wasn't sure. If she wanted him, fine — but he didn't want her to feel he'd bought her with gifts. *Oh, well.* Sharing the wagon seat, headed for the schoolhouse, with her on his arm . . . There couldn't be too much wrong, anyway.

"How are the new cattle doing?" she asked.

"Doing fine. They didn't lift their heads up from grazing the first seven days. They'll put on lots of weight."

"Aren't you worried? I mean going off up that trail . . . road?"

"We aren't the first. People been driving cattle up there since before the war. McCoy's trail is west of all those troublemakers in Kansas that you've heard about."

"But there's Indians."

"Indians just have to let us through. I'm not picking a fight with them, and I'll even pay them something, but word is if I give them a few head of cattle that will be enough."

He reined the horses down to a walk for the creek crossing. "Worst thing I can think of are the river crossings."

"Oh, I never even —"

"Well, there's plenty of rivers to cross,

and getting Hap's wagon over each one of them high and dry will be difficult. Steers can be cantankerous." He flicked the reins to make the team trot.

"People will talk about us," she said, not looking at him.

Ben nodded in the starlight that he heard her. "Talk all they want. When I get back from Kansas, we'll have us a wedding and a honeymoon."

"Where will we go on our honeymoon?"

"San Antonio? Austin?"

"Won't that be expensive?"

"I figure I'll be able to afford it by then."

"You really expect to make lots of money on this drive, don't you?"

"I've been planning on it, Jenny."

"I hope you aren't disappointed. I'd gladly be your wife if you weren't ever rich."

He looked at the stars peeking through the thin blanket of clouds. Somehow he had to make this trip a success or die trying. Her fingers tightened their grip on his arm; he looked down and smiled at her. *Somehow, Jenny, the drive will work.*

The day before New Year's Eve, Ben rode into town. He spotted the deputy coming down the boardwalk in front of the saddlery, and the man signaled that he wanted

161

to talk. Ben reined his horse over to stop before him.

"Coulter's been talking about you, Ben," Robert Kilmer said, taking off his felt hat and scratching his head.

"He needs me, he can find me." Ben checked his gray and reined him to a standstill.

"Trouble is, there's three now. His two brothers are with him."

"He crazy?"

Kilmer shrugged. "Says you showed him up in front of folks. Hurt his honor."

Ben squinted at the deputy. "He must be crazy. He was drunk as a hooter and got in my face. I just tossed him aside. Had better things to do than put up with a drunk."

"To hear him talk, you pistol-whipped him."

"Kilmer, the man's gone off the deep end. I hit him over the head when he wouldn't quit pestering me."

"He may be crazy, but he also might try something. Be careful. I've seen feuds like this start over nothing and end up with lots of good people getting killed."

"Hope he's got a funeral suit," Ben said, and booted the gray horse on toward the mercantile. His anger raged inside over the stupidity of the whole matter. He needed to order more supplies — at the end of the week they were going back to the border for the rest of the cattle.

Two hours later on his wide, circular ride, he stopped at Jenny's front door. He dismounted heavily and she came to the doorway with flour all over her hands.

"You caught me, Ben," she confessed, and smiled.

"How's that?" he asked, looking around the place.

"I wasn't expecting you so soon and about had an apple-raisin pie made."

"My favorite kind," he said, and swept off his hat. "I finished my business in town and rode out. Where's the boys?"

"Fishing. They shucked all the corn I needed for cornmeal and I let them have some time to be boys."

"Nice to do that," he said, and went to the fireplace. He heated his hands and backed up to the hearth. The warmth of the burning oak felt good radiating out at his back.

"Sometimes I worry my boys never have time to be boys."

"It's a busy world to grow up in."

"Too busy," she said, looking up from her dough rolling.

Ben took a straight-backed chair and sat

on it backward to watch her make her pies.

"I sure had fun at the dance," she said.

He nodded. He guessed everyone in the country knew about them and their intentions after the dance. It didn't bother him; in fact, he felt proud she'd accepted him. He could do a lot worse than marry her. There were times he wanted to go find a preacher and tie the knot — like this day, him sitting and watching her every move. It would be nice to have a woman of his own, especially her.

"Ben, I don't want to sound forward. . . ."

He looked up at her. "Yes?"

"We're both grown-ups, and I guess . . . well, we don't have to be married to be a couple."

He closed his eyes. "How would it look for me to come home to a wife who was with child?"

"It would be yours if it was so."

"Oh, Jenny." He rose and went to the small window and looked outside at the brown leaves dancing in a whirlwind. "It ain't what I want — I mean, I want you, but I don't want to ruin it." He wanted to say there was a chance that he might not even survive the drive. Then where would she be? They'd have lots of time together after the drive.

"The honeymoon?" she said, drying her hands.

"I'd like it to be perfect."

"I'll look forward to it, Ben."

He took her in his arms, kissed her, and kicked his conscience for building that barrier to what he felt in his arms. *Oh, cattle drive, fly by.*

When he released her, she spun around and looked whimsically at the open ceiling. "San Antonio. I like the sound of that."

He smiled. So did he.

Chapter 13

"You figure Martinez has those cattle for you?" Hap asked when they stopped for a break in midafternoon. Using the lee side of the wagon to escape the sand-stinging north wind howling around them, Ben and the crew ate Hap's fried apple pies for their midday meal.

Dru Nelson had finally shown up two days before they left for Mexico. The ex-soldier looked like he'd been on a three-week toot — but Ben needed the help and took him on anyway. How much booze could he find on the drive? Probably not much; the man had faced the same problem during the war. But drunks could always find it somewhere. Besides, when he was sober, Nelson took up grumbling most of the time.

"I figure the cattle will be there; Martinez needs the money," Ben answered Hap's question.

"Reckon he's still hooked up with Salano and his gang?"

"Miguel thinks Martinez owes that bandit

money, and Salano is looking out for himself; besides, getting his money and the cattle back, he'd make two profits." Ben finished his last bite of the pie.

"That makes sense. Want more? I've got plenty." Hap held out the Dutch oven, which was over half-full of them.

Ben shook his head. "No telling. But I'm counting on greed. He wants to sell me cattle, so I figure he'll have some there. They may not be what we need, but we may be forced to take them."

"Dealing with them greasers on the border is always risky," Dru Nelson said, helping himself to another pie.

Behind his salt-and-pepper beard, the man under the old blanket looked hard to Ben. Maybe he'd come on the drive because he'd worn out his welcome everywhere else. He'd due to watch. He hated that a loyal soldier had turned out that way, but he still had a cattle drive to organize and needed all hands to ever get the steers out of Texas and rolling north.

"How far you reckon them cattle we got at home will wander while we're down here?" Mark asked.

Ben turned up his jumper collar against the biting wind. "They'll likely stay up there in the hills. There's still plenty of grass and it's out of the wind. They shouldn't scatter too far."

"These new ones that hungry?"

"Mexicans ain't much on worrying about feed. I reckon there isn't much to eat where they bunch them. Being weak enough from starvation makes them easier to handle."

Mark looked off toward the south. "It takes all kinds, don't it?"

"Yes, and these are desperate times for many folks. Billy Jim, did you survive getting bucked off this morning?"

"That dang Willy Maker. He never got away, though." Billy Jim gave a sharp nod to punctuate his words.

"No, your catch rope works," Ben said, recalling how the lead rope the young cowboy kept tied to his belt saved the horse from running off. "Maybe you should trade him off for another?"

"Naw, I've got to learn how to ride them kind, too, to ever make a hand, Mr. Ben."

Ben nodded. "Let's saddle up, boys, and ride. Mexico's a day away and the sunlight's burning on these short days."

A chill went up his spine when he swung into the saddle; it drew goose bumps on his arms under his heavy shirt and jumper. He was headed for the unknown, and his success or failure depended on an unreliable source — Martinez.

The dull early-morning gleam of the river rushing over the shoal reflected the winter's weak sun. Ben, Chip, and Mark forded the river. Martinez must know they were there. They'd arrived in the late afternoon, set up camp, and posted guards. Miguel and Toledo had crossed over under the cover of night.

"They have a herd of smaller steers south of the village. Maybe five hundred," Miguel said. The campfire's light in the predawn reflected off his face. "Salano is not in town. We could not find out where he is, but they say he and some of his men rode out two days ago."

Ben nodded. "Any word on plans to take us?"

"I talked to a drunk *puta* in the cantina," Toledo said. "Her name was Duchess. She said that her boyfriend worked for Salano and they were gone to rob a stagecoach."

Ben smiled. "I hope she's right and they aren't but a few days' ride from here."

"She was very drunk." Toledo laughed. "I wanted to take her in back and ask her more, but she kept passing out."

"Sure," Chip said, clapping him on the shoulder. "We know what kind of questions

169

you'd have asked her back there."

Everyone laughed.

"You two boys did good. All of you keep a horse apiece saddled today; we may have to move in an instant. Can we take the herd if we need to and get them across?" Ben asked the pair.

"Oh, there are a few vaqueros with them."

"They tough *hombres?*" Ben asked.

Miguel shook his head. "I think they are only boys. They work cheap."

Hap came around with the coffeepot, filling cups. "You going to get Martinez out of bed?"

Ben nodded.

In the early-morning canted light, the three rode up the steep street into the village. Ben kept a wary eye out for any sign of trouble. The boys acted on edge, too. When they reached the cantina where Martinez roomed upstairs, Ben dismounted and handed Chip his reins.

"I'll try not to be long."

Hands on their gun butts, the boys nodded, looking around the narrow street, ready for anything.

Ben went up the staircase beside the building, reached the veranda, and knocked on the French door.

"Who is it?" Martinez hissed.

"Ben McCollough. Get up. We've got business to handle."

"Ah, *Señor* Ben, you are a week early." The man stood in a nightshirt, barefooted before him, rubbing his eyes. "Oh, what time is it?"

"Daytime. How many big steers do you have?"

"I have some good ones. Not *grande*, but they are good ones."

"How much are these runts?"

"Oh, I have to have three dollars apiece for them. They are hard to buy. Several gringos have been down here wanting cattle from me since I sold you your last ones."

"We had a deal last fall."

"Ah, but *señor*, it is a new year; I can't help the market has gone up. These cattle are worth a hundred dollars a head in Kansas."

Ben shook his head as the shorter man turned and started back into the room. "You are a damn long ways from there, and if they bring ten dollars, it won't hardly cover the expenses."

Martinez pointed at the ruffled front of his nightshirt. "I have expenses too."

"When can I go look at these small cattle?"

"Oh, tomorrow."

171

"What in the hell's wrong with today?"

"Oh, I have business with Don Querties." Martinez found a thin cigar butt in an ashtray and lit it with shaky hands.

"No! You've got business with me." If Salano was out of town, they needed to move before he came back.

"But my word —"

"Get dressed; we're riding out there and looking at those steers."

Martinez rubbed the backs of his arms. "Cold in here, isn't it?"

"You're going to be cold riding out there in that nightshirt. I'm going to have the boys go get your buggy. Where's it at?"

"The stables."

Ben walked across the room and onto the balcony. "Go get Martinez's buggy at the stables. We're going out to look at the cattle soon as he gets dressed."

"Tina! Tina!" Martinez shouted. "Where are my clothes?"

A teenage girl came running and threw open the wooden wardrobe. From it she tossed onto the bed a shirt and pants. Then, hands on her hips, she glared at him. "What else you want?"

When he reached for her, she shunned his advance and headed for the door to the adjoining room. "What else you want?"

"Ah, my darling, I want your lovely body, of course." He pulled the nightshirt off over his head, revealing that he wore no underwear.

She wrinkled her nose in disgust at him exposing himself to her and left the room.

"She loves me," Martinez said, and pulled on his pants.

Ben doubted that, but held his comments to himself. He felt antsy to get out to the herd, look them over, and get the deal made. His biggest dread concerned the size of these animals. Miguel had already warned him this bunch wasn't like those stout steers he had bought the first time.

Martinez stood in the buggy an hour later, extolling the virtues of the longhorn steers in the herd. Ben ignored him and pushed Roan through them. They were southern cattle, not much coat, and most were hardly more than two-year-olds — younger than he wanted to handle, but perhaps all he could get. There were other cattle dealers along the border, but the other drovers had already been there, or so Martinez said.

"Dollar a head."

"Oh, no!" Martinez slapped his forehead and knocked off his flat-brimmed black hat. "You steal them from me. That wouldn't buy a goat."

"I ain't buying goats. I'm buying your runty steers."

"*Señor* Ben, look at them."

Ben drew up his horse and put both hands on the saddle horn. "I've looked at the damn things. I'm willing to pay a dollar a head."

"No way." Martinez dropped his head in defeat. "Ben, let us go find Tina and have us some *huevos* and frijoles and tequila. She's nice, no? Oh, Ben, she is like velvet in the bed. I give her to you. Oh, *Señor* Ben, let us party a few days. Have us a *grande* time, no, *mi amigo?* You don't like Tina, I get another nice one for you. You like them fat or with big ones?"

"Martinez, get hold of yourself. I came down here to buy cattle, not mess around and party. I've got business at home. Now these cheap cattle aren't worth half what those big steers were."

"But these ones cost much more money."

"You never paid the catchers any more."

"More expensive — oh, you don't know —"

"Damn it, I'll pay you a dollar-fifty a head."

"Two dollars."

"A buck-fifty."

"Take them day after tomorrow?"

"No, today — I've sent Mark after the crew."

"Today!" Martinez searched around as if looking for help besides the barefooted boys dressed in shorts despite the cold wind, sitting on their skinny horses waiting for his orders.

"Solano isn't here," Ben said. "He's off robbing stagecoaches."

Martinez blinked at him in disbelief. Ben looked away smothering a grin. He knew more about the man's partner than he did.

"Get down to cases. A dollar and a half a head."

"Ben," the man cried. "I must go eat something. My stomach hurts so. I have to have two dollars. No less or I lose my life; it is at stake here. I owe so much money."

"I'll only pay that for sound ones; you throw in the culls."

Martinez made a face and crawled up into the buggy seat looking pale as a ghost. "I am sick; you've made me sick to my stomach."

"I'm making you rich." Ben looked off to the north, hoping for sight of his crew. He intended to be long gone before the bandits returned.

Martinez at last sent one of his young herders to find him some food. Holding his stomach, he groaned as if in pain. "Stealing my cattle. I may never, ever recover from this." More moaning. "Who will you buy cattle from then?"

"Salano?" Ben said, and booted his horse off to look some more at the herd. He'd had a belly full of Martinez and wouldn't be standing around there if he didn't absolutely need this bunch. Reining Roan through them, he tried to spot the weaker ones. There would be some. If he could make a mental note of the bad ones' description, he could cut them at the counting point.

Where were those boys?

The crew arrived and the counting began despite Martinez's efforts to divert them. Ben pointed out the bad ones, and Digger either roped and dragged them aside or Mark cut them back and drove them to the side bunch.

Ben also noticed that Mark was learning to heel-rope the steers that Digger caught, so the black youth could get his head rope off the cattle easier. His cattle counter, Billy Jim, sat his horse, and nothing distracted his counting of the passing animals.

Martinez sat rejected in the buggy, feeding his face on the enormous amount of food a fat woman delivered to him. Ben had no time for him. The boys were doing a good job and things were going smoothly — so far. Inside of an hour, they'd be across the river and trailing the herd north. But he'd better get this business over with and not count his chickens until they hatched.

"Four hundred fifty-six good ones," Billy Jack reported when the last steer danced by him.

"How many culls, Mark?"

"Thirty-seven."

Hap handed him the sack of gold coins from his saddlebags. Ben nodded. "Get them moving; I can catch up."

"Four hundred fifty-six is my count. What did you get?" Ben asked.

Martinez shook his head as if it made no difference.

"Thirty-seven culls."

"Pay me."

"Nine hundred and twelve dollars," Ben said, and dismounted to count out the coins.

"I am ruined. No matter," Martinez said, and shook his head.

"Next time you make a deal, you better know your expenses."

"Next time? There will be no next time."

"That's your business," Ben said, and began making stacks of the coins on the floor of the buggy: nine of a hundred, then twelve dollars more. He pulled the drawstring tight on his canvas sack of money.

"*Señor?*"

Ben turned.

"May God be with you all the way to Kansas." Martinez made the sign of a cross.

"We'll need him," Ben said, and booted Roan for the river.

At the river's edge he watched several of the steers jump off into a few inches of water, land, then, shock-faced, wade on across. They didn't know what a river meant — they came from down in the real Mexican desert.

"Help, help, I'm drowning!"

Ben whirled Roan around. Dru Nelson was in the river downstream from the ford, flailing water with his hands and his feet like a paddleboat.

Chip rode down the sandy bank, headed for him. Then he reined up his horse and shook his head before he started back out. "Stand up, asshole. It's only waist-deep where you're at."

The boys obviously had no love for the ex-soldier. He'd have to make his own way to Kansas, from the sounds of things. When Ben glanced back, the thoroughly soaked Nelson looked bedraggled, leading his horse and wading for shore.

It would be a long trek, too.

Chapter 14

With night guards — and armed ones — they made the trip without incident or sign of the bandits. Ben felt relieved coming off the grade for the home place. The wagon rattled along and the team of horses within sight of the home corrals picked up speed.

"You ready for those mules?" Ben shouted over at Hap.

"Hell, no, but I'll need them." Hap gave a wry scowl at him.

"Digger says they're ready to pull the wagon. Him and Billy Jim are going to hook them up in the morning."

"Bless them two. You know," Hap yelled over the harness jingle, pounding hooves, and the wagon's familiar knocks and rattles, "you are damn lucky to gather up that many kids and them make a crew."

"We are, Hap. We really are."

"I can handle things; you still got a couple hours' daylight — why don't you ride over and see her?" Hap asked.

"I better clean up first."

"Don't take long." Hap laughed as he rode on. "Tell her I said howdy. I kinda miss taking her deer and eating her pie."

Ben waved that he heard him and loped for the house.

When he came outside in his clean clothes, the boys already had Roan brushed and saddled. They all sat around and nodded when he told them to listen to Hap; then he mounted Roan and started out.

A half dozen hats sailed underneath him and the gelding began to crow-hop, bucking, kicking, and jumping. Ben managed to head him for the gate, pulling leather and reins. The men's hurrahs were loud and full of laughter. They did it on purpose. He'd teach those pups a lesson or two.

"Damn it, Roan, quit!" But the horse didn't stop humping his back until Ben let him run.

He crossed Dry Creek and started up the wagon tracks cut into the brown grass. Busy considering where to move the herd for more grass, Ben looked up in time to see someone rein his horse back in the cedars. Cold chills ran down the sides of his face, and he turned Roan off into the dense evergreens. Was it one of Coulter's men? The man carried a rifle. Ben dismounted, hitched Roan to a bough, hung his spurs on the horn, and started uphill on foot with the .44 in his fist.

Maybe he was getting paranoid. No, this bunch of hardheads needed a lesson or two. There was no way he intended to spend the rest of his life looking over his shoulder for the next one. He'd heard about these family feuds — wiping out everyone on both sides in back-shooting episodes.

He paused to listen. Above him he heard the impatient horse stomping around. He moved swiftly, coming around the curtain of cedars and behind the horse and rider.

"Get your hands up and drop that rifle." The Colt in his hand was cocked and ready.

"Huh?"

"Drop it or die!"

Seconds ticked by, as if the man wanted to consider his chances of whirling around and firing. Then his shoulders slumped and he dropped the rifle and raised his hands.

"What's your name?"

"Sam."

"Sam Coulter?"

"Yeah."

"Get off that horse."

"Go ahead and shoot me. Get it over with."

"Coulter, I don't know what your trouble is, but if you ain't got any more to do than sit and wait to ambush me, you need something to do." Ben jerked his handgun out of the man's holster and stuck it into his waistband.

"Huh?"

He guessed Coulter's age as early twenties. He had blue eyes and light-colored hair that came to his shoulders and needed a currycomb taken to it.

"Take off those boots. Maybe a barefoot walk home will convince you I mean business." Ben searched around. No telling where the others were.

"You think that'll stop us?"

"Next time wear your best suit."

"Huh?"

" 'Cause I'd hate for the county to have to bury you in those rags. Get those boots off."

Ben waited until he had them off. "All right, which way are you going?"

"South." Coulter pointed in that direction, looking confused, standing in his holey gray socks.

"Start running. You don't run fast enough, I intend to shoot you in the foot."

"I'm leaving!"

Ben watched as he holstered his own Colt and drew Coulter's out. Taking careful aim, he fired a round after the fleeing bushwhacker that kicked up dust to the right and drew more speed from him.

Crying and groaning, Coulter disappeared off the hillside. Ben picked up the rifle, jammed it in the boot, climbed on Roan, and led the bay horse behind. He didn't want Coulter to have a chance to ride. He'd turn the animal loose before he got to Jenny's and the pony should go home. The firearms he planned to keep.

He needed to know more about the Coulters. If they were that dead-set on revenge, he needed to convince them otherwise or eliminate them. Most of all he worried about Jenny and her boys while they were gone north with the drive. She didn't need any trouble either.

He set the bay horse loose a few miles short of her place. Without his bridle and with a hard lash on his butt, the bay tore out for parts unknown. Coulter would be lucky to have a saddle left.

"Ben, you're back." Jenny rushed out carrying her skirt and hugged him when he rode up to her house. "Did you have any trouble?"

"No," he said, smelling her clean hair and still wondering how to handle the Coulter mess. Damn, he needed to do something.

"I'll have supper in an hour. The boys will be in from chores. Can you stay?" she asked.

Ben stayed longer than he intended. Jenny's company had grown to have a settling effect on him. Somehow, with her, he felt free — the worries of the cattle drive, the Coulters' threats, all flew away, and his money worries even evaporated.

Her boys in the loft asleep, she sat upon his lap in the straight-backed chair. He wondered where she had been all his life as he hugged her and they kissed sweetly. Their intimate closeness aroused him, but he knew that he could contain it — until he returned. Then the image of the blue-eyed Coulter with his long mane and scraggly facial hair made him want to shudder.

Chapter 15

The next morning Ben spoke to his crew. "I want to warn you: Somehow I'm embroiled in a feud. Harold Coulter, any of you know him?"

Mark nodded. The others shook their heads.

"Anyway, he and his brothers are out to kill me. They've shot at me from ambush, and yesterday one of his brothers was waiting to back-shoot me on the creek road. All I know that I ever did to them was toss Harold Coulter aside when he was drunk."

"They're a mean bunch," Mark said. "That Harold bothered my maw until she got out the shotgun."

"He did?" Ben frowned. That was the first he'd heard anything about her and Coulter.

"She didn't want nothing to do with him."

"I understand," Ben said. Maybe that shed some light on the matter; he'd never spoken to her about Coulter. Perhaps this

185

whole feud was more over Jenny than the bar incident.

"Boys, we need to divide up forces. Mark, you choose three hands. Move the herd west, easy-like. Keep them off those German farms out there. Take a packhorse and some food. I'll be by to check on you if you have troubles, and I'll send replacements in a week. Chip and Digger have the horse- and mule-breaking detail."

"I'll go with the herd," Dru said.

Ben nodded. "Who else, Mark?"

"Billy Jim."

"Whew," the full-faced youth said in relief. "Thought you'd never ask."

"Toledo, you and Miguel help Chip with the horses. We need lots of that salt taken out of them. Any questions?"

"Mr. Ben, when we leaving for Kansas?" Toledo asked.

"Early March, when the grass begins to green up. My daddy always said spring moved north fifteen miles a day. That's about our speed."

"Yes, sah."

Ben went back to the house for another cup of coffee. He shouted to Mark, "Take along this rifle I got yesterday. There's a carton of cartridges for it in here, too."

"I'll get it."

Ben nodded, then went in for his coffee and a talk with Hap.

"I've got the panniers filled for them. Billy Jim can probably cook anything they need. That boy's going to make a hand," Hap said, rolling out pie dough.

Ben searched around to be certain they were alone. "Yeah. Mark told me this morning that Coulter tried to court his mother and she ran him off with a shotgun."

"Well, kiss my toe." Hap shook his head. "She ever tell you that?"

"No, but I've never mentioned my problems with him. Didn't want her upset."

"I could never figure how a man that drunk felt all out of place over you tossing him aside." He sprinkled more flour on the dough through his fingers and then rolled it flatter. "Just didn't make sense."

Ben walked to the window and watched Mark and Billy Jim saddling the packhorse. "You remember Dru being that sour when we were in the army?"

"No, he's became an old drunk since he came home. His wife said she thought he was killed and ran off with another guy while he was gone. Wouldn't come back either after he located her."

"He wasn't the only one lost his wife over the war."

"Guess it strikes us all different."

"I guess," Ben said, finishing his coffee. "I'll help the boys move this new herd out with the rest of them."

"Ride careful, and watch out for them Coulters."

"I'll be back late tonight, unless things go well."

"Hey, they must have those mules hitched to the wagon, from all the commotion going on," Hap said, clapping the flour off his hands and heading for the open door.

Both men stood outside. Digger was on the seat, lines in his hand. A cowboy apiece held on to each mule's head.

"Let 'em go!" Digger shouted.

The mules took off in a stiff-legged trot, then tried to run. But Digger's feet jammed against the dash and rearing back on the lines was holding a portion of their haste down.

"Don't ruin my wagon!" Hap shouted through cupped hands, then shook his head. "Never heard a word I said."

"He did," Ben said, and headed for the pens to get a horse for himself.

Clouds coming spoke of rain. Things were greening up every warm spell; Ben felt good about the coming drive. Why, it would be over before he knew about it. The steer weren't exactly what he had in mind. Half should do well — the smaller end would be harder to sell unless they grew like rank weeds between then and when they got there. Some tallow on all of them would help.

In the afternoon warmth, he spotted a big reddish-brown steer hike up his back leg and toss his head as far as he could reach to lick a spot on his back. The hair curled under the animal's tongue, and Ben smiled. A sure sign cattle were on the mend was when they licked themselves and the hair curled. He headed for the smoke of Billy Jim's fire.

"How's things going, Billy?"

"Fine, sir."

"You ain't ready to quit, are you?" Ben asked, squatting down on his boot heels.

"Naw, not me." The youth shook his head and stirred rice in boiling water.

"Good. Hap says you're a good cook."

Billy about blushed. "I got a question to ask." He looked all around to be certain no one else was within hearing range."

"What's that?"

"The first time you ever went in one of those cathouses, afterwards did you keep thinking you should go back and marry her?"

"Yeah." Ben shook his head. "But you

can't. She won't, and that's life."

"Been a bothering me a lot. I'm proud you answered me."

"I've had the same feelings myself. It'll wear off in time." Ben clapped him on the shoulder. Millescent had torn him up worse than any woman on earth, and he had been a grown man by then.

"You must of had fun?" Ben said.

"Oh, man, that Miguel knew all of them, ah, doves, and he showed us a real good time." Billy Jim's face glowed and he checked on the coffeepot. "Want some before you ride back?"

"No, I better get back. Good luck. Keep an eye out for trouble."

"We've got that Winchester right over there," Billy Jim said, and went back to stoking his fire.

With the sunset at his back, Ben headed back for headquarters.

The steers acted calm enough once the fighting and jostling was over between individuals in both herds to see who was top steer and the rest under him sorted out their order.

Eight weeks and they'd be moving out. He could hardly wait, and yet dread filled his mind of the things unplanned, things not yet thought of to do before leaving. The time would pass fast enough. He needed to take Jenny's boys out and introduce them to his cow-calf herd scattered in the hills. They should have no trouble — most would be calved — save bringing back to his home range some wanderers. So far the mother cows had stayed clear of the big herd and kept to themselves, a fact he appreciated. Cutting anything out of the steers would be a tough job.

After dark he dropped from the saddle and smiled at Hap in his white apron standing in the lighted doorway.

"You damn near missed eating tonight."

He chuckled at his friend's words and turned the unsaddled gray into the trap to roll his itchy back in the dust.

"I'm ready. Steers are settled in out there," Ben said.

"Maybe they'll get used to thunder then. I figure some of them steers never been in a thunderstorm in their life down there on the border."

"Has it been that long since it rained down there, you mean?"

"Burned-uppest country I ever saw."

Ben poured himself a cup of coffee, noticing it was freshly made. "Pretty dry down there." He blew on the steam. "Boys doing fine today?"

"Sure, they're hustling on them horses, and Digger's got them mules so they whoa and go."

"I'll take Toledo and Miguel to check cows in the morning if it ain't raining."

"Good idea. But I doubt that you get to go."

Ben nodded. During the night he woke to hear the drum of rain on the shingles and the low growl of thunder off in the distance. He wondered about Mark and his crew, then turned over and went back to sleep.

Chapter 16

"I never encouraged him," Jenny said. "He came by once and stopped to water his horse. Asked if he could buy some food, and I shook my head. To turn a hungry man away is against my raising. He acted polite enough.

"So I fixed him a plate and he bragged on the cold food the entire time he sat on my porch and ate it. I guess I should have taken heed of that. I thought he was only being polite.

"Then he came back again and I still was polite." She shook her head and turned her lips inward to wet them. Then with a sigh she went on. "He asked me to the schoolhouse dance and I said no. He became quite bossy and I reached inside the door and brought out the shotgun."

"Mark said you had to drive him off."

"That wasn't enough for him. I met him the next time he rode in and ordered him off the place. This time I gave him some birdshot to send him on his way."

"He hasn't been back?"

"No, he knows I wouldn't use birdshot the next time."

Ben reached out and hugged her to his chest. "I'm sorry, Jenny. I didn't want to upset you, but he's mad at me over the whole thing, I guess."

"Oh, Ben, I'm so sorry."

"No, I'll settle with Harold Coulter before I leave here."

"Sun's come out," she said, obviously to change the subject. "Let's go out and see the rainbow. There must be one out there."

With her under his arm, they stood in the wet yard with water rushing off the ground in thin sheets and they searched the butter-milk sky.

"There it is, Ben." She pointed at the great arch.

He hugged her shoulders and kissed her forehead. "We should go see if the pot of gold's there."

"Yes."

Her sons came out of the barn and she pointed the rainbow out to them.

"Everyone ready for lunch?" she asked her men.

"Starved, ain't you, Mr. Ben?" Tad asked, and smiled at them.

"I can sure eat," Ben agreed.

"We about have the harnesses all oiled,

and the saddles too," the younger one, Ivory, reported.

Ben nodded in approval. "First day it doesn't rain you can come over and we'll check cows together."

"That's a deal. It'll beat doing chores around here."

"Oh, surely you can get them done before you ride over?" he asked.

"We sure can," Ivory said as they washed up on the porch.

When Ben returned to the ranch after sundown, the wind had switched out of the north and the clouds cleared to reveal all the stars. The three jaded horses tied to the hitching rack bothered him, and he swung down at the house.

The sight of Mark's hatless face in the light from the doorway knifed him.

"What's happened?"

"Six guys rode up and started to stampede the steers by shooting off pistols."

"You know them?"

"Think they were Coulters. I'm not sure," Mark said with some effort. "Billy Jim got two of them with that rifle."

"Bill, you all right?" Ben asked, seeing him sitting at the table.

"You said it wouldn't be no Sunday-school picnic," Bill said, and bobbed his head, looking upset.

"Where are they?"

"We brought their bodies in." Mark shrugged and looked warily across the table at Ben. "Didn't know what we should do with them. Dru said we had to take them to the law."

With a nod of approval to the unspeaking veteran seated at the end of the table, Ben surveyed the rest of the crew standing around in the candlelit room. "It's the best thing to do. You did right. How about the steers?"

"They never did much. They're fine."

"Chip, in the morning you and the others take a turn at guarding. We'll ride into town with the bodies. Any more of them get shot up?"

"Yeah, but his horse fell and he got on behind someone else and they cut a trail," Dru said.

Ben could see the man's hands were trembling and that he tried to hide them. "Hap, get Dru a drink. In fact, we could all use a shot of whiskey."

"Yeah, we've been snakebit," Billy Jim said, looking around at the others.

His humor drew some chuckles, and Ben gave him a nod.

Past noon they reined up before Deputy Kilmer's small frame house and dismounted heavily. The two corpses were wrapped in canvas and bound tight with rope. Each one was belly-down over an MC horse. Kilmer came out of the house with a frown at their obvious cargo.

"Howdy, Ben; what's happened?"

"Some jaspers jumped my crew and got lead instead of my steers."

"Who are they?"

"We think Coulters or their kin."

Kilmer removed his hat and scratched the thin hair on top. "Damn, they've lost their minds over this feud business."

"Lost their lives too," Ben said.

"You know them?"

"Boys guessed they were all Coulters."

"Take them down to Yancy's. He can hold them for a day. Then they go in the ground if unclaimed. Need to file a report. You shoot them, Ben?"

"No. Billy Jim can tell you the details."

"Need you to come along and answer some questions. Ben, you come inside too. Damn, those fools have lost their minds."

Ben had to agree as he turned to Mark. "I guess you two can take them to Yancy's. That be okay?"

"Sure," the lawman said, and Ben gave Mark and Dru a head toss to take the bodies away. "Tell Yancy I want their names, if he can get them."

"We will," Mark said. And they rode on with the two bodies.

After all the papers were filled out, Kilmer walked them to the front door. "I swear, Ben, that bunch is dumber than I don't know what."

"You can understand I'm tired of messing with them."

"Ben, I understand. My hands are tied. I could bring them in for attempted rustling, but I doubt I could get it to stick for long. Bill, you take care, young man."

"I will, sir," the youth said, and sprang into the saddle.

"We'll handle our part," Ben said; then the two of them rode to the gun shop. He checked on the rifles; they hadn't arrived.

"I'm buying the beer, and we're eating off the free lunch counter across the street, guys," Ben announced when he came outside and all his hands were waiting at the hitching rail.

Ben ordered the beer at the bar and looked over at Billy Jim studying the famous nude painting that hung on the wall over the mirror.

"Never seen the lady before?" Ben asked.

"Nope." Billy Jim shook his head. "Second time I've ever been in a saloon. First time was down there in Mexico."

"Lunch is on the counter," Ben said, and they ambled over.

"Well, stranger," Milly said from the curtained doorway. "You're getting to be a real stay-at-home kind of guy."

Ben looked at her. She wore her dress made of lace veils and leaned her shoulder against the facing. He nodded. "Good place to be."

After an "oh well" look at the tin ceiling tiles, she smiled big at the others. "You boys are working for the meanest boss in the county. I was you, I'd go find me a real job."

She tossed a strip of the lace over her shoulder and went off into the back with a harrumph of disapproval.

"You know her?" Billy Jim asked, holding his heaping plate and looking at the dancing curtain she flipped going away.

"Milly," Ben said, looking hard at the dusty, stuffed bison head on the wall. Milly was good enough. Damn her, she could put a verbal knife in anyone. He could regret all he wanted — he'd learned all about her and her wanton ways. She was exactly what she wanted to be — a strumpet who used men for her own satisfaction.

The food wadded up in his mouth. He needed a fresh perspective. An image of Jenny, pushing back an errant wave of hair, smiling at his approach, took all the sourness away. Thank God he had Jenny, and she would be his wife one day next fall. Good enough. He washed the rye bread, German sausage, and hard cheese down with the foamy draft beer.

Chapter 17

Barrels of flour, baking powder, rice, beans, sugar, salt, pepper, dried chili peppers, a roll of canvas, two spools of new rope, harness repairs, dried apples, raisins — the list went on and on. Hap even named the mules: Matthew, John, Luke, and Cyrus. Cyrus because they already had a Mark, he said. The days began to lengthen and the wild oats were making the steers' hides sparkle.

Ben dropped in to see Jenny. Her sons ready to look after the MC mother cows and calves in his absence, he and Jenny went walking through her blooming peach orchard. The pink blossoms made the trees look like bouquets.

"You leaving next week?" she asked quietly.

"Figure we have one more frost. Always get a cold snap to test the peaches, don't we?"

She sighed and then agreed. "Yes, we usually do. But I hope I have enough of them put up to make you pie for the rest of the year when you get back."

"I'd sure not complain."

"You never complain much for a man."

"Don't do much good. Can't fix it, ride on."

"Ben, I'll be praying for you."

"Jenny, that's good. Those boys and I will need all the help we can get. But we'll make it."

"So that you come back to me."

He hugged her shoulder. "Wild horses couldn't keep me away."

"I wasn't worried about wild horses." She laughed and they walked on in the warming sun.

There was no sign of the Coulters. The notion that no one had heard anything about them niggled Ben. It was like they had vanished off the edge of the earth, but he knew better, and the feud issue wasn't over.

All the steers bore a fresh bar behind their left shoulder as the trail brand. Ben figured with the tally at eight hundred and sixty he should get there with eight hundred, if they didn't have too many stampedes or losses crossing flood-swollen rivers. His tally book showed two had died, and fifty were left on the ranch with his MC brand on them, either too small or not suitable for the trail drive.

Digger was due back from San Antonio. He promised to find someone to help Hap and to wrangle horses. So when Ben saw the familiar sombrero of the black cowboy appear coming across the meadow with someone else on a small horse, he figured his wrangler had arrived.

"Mr. Ben, sir, this here be Lou Song."

"Howdy, Lou Song," Ben said to the Asian youth, who nodded, looking pleased, sitting on his thin bay horse. Dressed in threadbare clothing, he wore a skullcap and had a short queue. The boy was hardly five foot tall, and Ben wondered how good he'd be at horse wrangling.

"He the horse wrangler?" Ben asked.

"Lou Song is a good hand with hosses. He ain't afraid to work either."

"Me pleased if you hire me, Mr. Ben."

"Digger says you can handle horses and help Hap. It's fine with me."

"Good deal. When we start work?"

"Right now, we're loading, Digger can show you a bunk. We'll be moving out in a few days."

Digger dropped out of the saddle and readjusted his chaps and pants. "I guess I never thanked you for buying me these clothes in Mexico, Mr. Ben."

"Oh, how is that?"

"Well, they treated me a lot different in San Antonio when I was barefooted and in overalls."

"I bet they did." Ben laughed and clapped him on the shoulder. He'd bet that pistol-toting, black cowboy did draw some respect.

So his army of misfits prepared for the final day. Neighbors dropped by to wish him luck, and ladies left pies and cakes. A few even hinted to try to find out his intentions toward Jenny, but all they got out of Ben was, "She's a mighty fine lady, and anyone gets her will be proud."

Men warned him about the treachery they'd face in the Indian Nation. Others spoke of late snows in Kansas that might wipe out the herd, leaving this early. Ben heard of a monster story for every day he figured they'd be on the road to reach Joe McCoy's shipping pens.

"Them bushwhackers are still up there," Harley Miner said. The lean-faced rancher squatted on his boot heels beside Ben. "They jumped the McEntosh boys near some springs and horsewhipped Denton. Took the whole herd. Them boys came back busted. Lost everything. Ben, it's a terrible risk you're taking."

"We aren't going in that Baxter Springs country. Going west. Some part-Cherokee named Chisholm has a trading post on the Arkansas Fork. We cross the river there. That's miles west of those bushwhackers, and McCoy's man is plowing a furrow right now down from Abilene to show us the way. I have the letter in my pocket."

"Yeah, but those deals are never like they're told."

"I don't know about the forecast price of steers. I'm certain they embellish that some, but cattle aren't worth nothing here."

"Still, I admire your nerve. God be with you, Ben McCollough. You may be on the right track for all of us."

Ben nodded, and the two shook hands. Harley departed with his wife in their buckboard.

"You reckon if all these folks had any sand in their craws they'd get off their butts and head a bunch north?" Hap asked, joining him.

"It's the unknown, Hap. Trail gets cut in, it will be like Columbus when he came here. They say his men thought they'd fall off the end of the earth. Now look — folks go all over on the ocean."

"That's us sailing over the sea of grass."

"You're right. How's the new boy working out?"

"Good, he can handle horses. Never seen one of them celestials could do that. He knows lots about cooking, too."

"I figured Digger knew we didn't need anyone couldn't pull his weight."

"I hate we hired that Dru, though," Hap said. "He don't fit. Nothing but a drunk drying out. Grouchy as a damn bear, too."

"Too late now. He'll do his work. Don't expect that fresh face and willingness you get from the boys."

"I damn sure won't get it from him," Hap said, and headed back for the house.

Ben saddled the gray for his last trip over to see Jenny before he left. He rode him by the house, told Hap he'd be back, and left in a high lope. The trip over proved uneventful, and he found her in a rocking chair sewing on her wedding dress.

She rose at the sight of him and ran to hide it.

"Hope it won't be bad luck," she said, coming outside. "It's supposed to be bad luck for the groom to see the dress before the wedding."

"That's for young people." Ben chuckled, swept her up in his arms, and kissed her. He felt sick even before he took his lips from hers. How he would miss her warmth and fine spirits — but then, too, the knowledge that she was waiting for his return would hasten the days.

"You and the boys be careful," he told her. "No word from anywhere about those Coulters does not set well with me. They're out there. Don't take chances."

"He won't hurt me. I showed him it was over."

"Be careful," Ben whispered in her ear.

"For you I will," she said, and hugged him tight.

Cattle bawled and the riders came in from all directions, bringing in the stragglers to the main herd and shaping them to move out. In the predawn's pinkish-purple light and cool air, a jumper felt good to Ben as he worked Roan moving cattle. Hap and Lou Song were rolling.

Those two were already on the move with the half-broken mules and the remuda of loose horses. They'd set up camp that night at Willow Crossing, ten miles north.

Five days from that morning they'd cross the Brazos above the town of Waco, if they had any luck. North of Fort Worth and the Trinity he aimed to put some more weight on them in the tall-grass prairie, if someone hadn't burned it off. There would be some strong grass up there. His slick steers looked and acted good. The six weeks of grazing and herding had solved lots of the problem of mixing cattle and hitting the trail — that unsettled business about who was the kingpin in this crowd had been long ago decided.

He never forgot they still were wild animals drug out of the brush to be branded and castrated as calves — some even later in life than that — then rounded up after playing deer for a few years in the thorny thickets of Mexico. Still, as they lined out in a string over a half mile long, he felt good. They were headed for Abilene. *Col. Joe McCoy, get the gates ready.*

His swing riders learned how to make the serpentine delivery so the cattle didn't push the leaders in the river, but spread them out down the bank by forming a parallel bunch to the riverbank.

Ben spent hours in the saddle, riding ahead, leaving white rags to wave in mesquite trees and point the way. They had two days of rain beyond Waco. It soaked man and beast in the cold downpours. The camp wood smoked and hardly made heat enough to cook, much less drive the chill out of his men.

"I hope it never, ever rains again," Chip said, dropping out of the saddle.

"Better not wish that," Ben said. "Dust'd be so bad it would hide you."

"Guess you're right, but I'd like to be dry for a while so my fingers didn't look all shriveled up like prunes."

"We'll find that dry weather, too," Dru said. "Man's a plumb fool to ever be a damn drover. Only old folks and young ones sign on."

"You should know," Chip said and went on to where Hap had a canvas stretched tree to tree to shelter from some of the precipitation.

"Well, I ain't still wet behind the ears."

"Well, I ain't a damn drunk shaking like a dog passing peach seeds either."

"Cut it out, boys," Ben said after them. "This job's tough enough. Don't make each other mad."

"You said this would be no Sunday-school picnic," Billy Jim said, dismounting his horse with rain running off the brim of his sodden hat.

"Guess I was right."

"How far is the Red River, Mr. Ben?"

"A good ways. Why?"

"Times I get that feeling you mentioned."

"Of going back?"

"Yes, sir. But I ain't. They tell me them gals in Abilene are the prettiest in the world."

"Since Mexico you got kind of an eye out for womenfolks, ain't you?"

Billy Jim sucked on an eyetooth and nodded. "Mighty fine thing."

Ben agreed. He only hoped his own was safe and dry. He worked his stiff fingers. Chip was right: It'd be nice when his fingers weren't all shriveled up.

They skirted settlements and plowed fields. Ben made certain there was water and wood. The sun finally shone, but the north wind that drove the rain out of Texas had a nip that made the cowboys ride under blankets for warmth.

"Too hot and too cold. Why can't it be spring and nice?" Hap looked up from stirring his beans.

"It'll do that too," Ben promised, coming after coffee after getting in from his morning ride to find a place to camp.

"When?"

"Next couple days. Tomorrow we'll be across the Trinity and you can make a list of the things you need from town. We'll heal up on the tall grass for a week. We may be pushing spring a little."

"Good, 'cause them boys are getting

worn out, herding all day and only getting a half night's sleep."

"Part of the deal, Hap."

"We camp here a week, it'll take the month of April to cross the Indian Nation, right?"

"That's what I had allotted."

"Then two to three weeks to get to Abilene?"

"Close."

Hap looked at his X's in the calendar. "There any chance I'd be back in San Antonio on the Fourth of July?"

"You might be, why?"

"Lou Song told me they're going to have the biggest fireworks show they've ever had there this year."

"Be something to see."

"Well." Hap put the pencil and calendar away in his small writing desk. "I ain't no kid. I can live without fireworks."

"Good." Ben smiled. His old noncom made a great guy, and on the move he was less sarcastic than at home. Why, it had been days since he used that "Benjamin McColloughie, you listen here" routine on him.

After a week camped on the Trinity, the cowboys took baths, a shiny, snow-white operation that would have blinded any on-lookers. They also washed their clothes and hung them on the brush to dry while they sunbathed in their ivory splendor. Everyone but Dru regained a better disposition.

Heading north again, Ben located a ferry to take the wagon across the Red River, and they finally started for the Indian line. The plan was to head the steers into the river and hope the big black lead steer they called Stonewall Jackson would swim to the far shore with little encouragement.

"Boys, if those cattle ever get to swimming in a circle, you get out of their way. That river has no bottom and it's full of quicksand. We get messed up in it we can lose cattle — that's money, but worse than that, we can lose lives." Ben shook his head. "We need to trust Stonewall."

"I think he'll do like he did at Waco," Mark said. "Aim him for that bank and he'll go."

"Yes, I agree. Dru, you go with the wagon, take you a horse, and meet us on the far side," Ben said.

The man nodded that he heard him.

"Lou Song, can you swim?"

"Swim, me no drown, bossy man."

"Good. We'll take the horses across first thing. Them over there might help encourage the steers to go to them."

"Mr. Ben, we've been crossing rivers since we left home. What's so bad about this one?" Billy Jim asked.

"Trust me; we won't have many tougher ones than the Red."

"I'll be ready then."

"Good," Ben said.

"Chip, it's up to you and Mark to get them started. But swim your horses wide. We ever get them started and they keep going, we may make it."

From where he sat the gray, he could see all the trees and debris that clogged the river, the reddish-brown water moving to his right at a good enough clip for him to know the stock would land farther downstream rather than directly across from him. The white-barked sycamores were not budded out yet; a few elms had broken dormancy. The river would be cold, and the entire matter of a safe crossing made his stomach churn.

"Bring the horses," he said, and they drove the remuda down the draw. A big black horse took the lead and set out to swim it; the others hesitated and had to be choused in by the cowboys. Then they all were swimming, with Lou Song clinging to his saddle horn on the upstream side, his horse making the swim easy. The black climbed up the bank and Lou shouted for him to go on. He stopped to shake, and that made a backup in the ones behind. They'd soon all be in the quicksand and bogged down.

Ben jerked out his Colt and fired it in the air. The black bolted and the others never hesitated. They piled up the bank and were on the grassy flat high above the river when Lou rounded them up.

"See what we must do?" Ben shouted to Chip and Mark. "You get a backup and the river will be full of cattle. Both of you stay on the upstream side crossing and get over there. We need them to run out of the way."

"We see, Ben," Mark shouted back.

"Let's roll them," Ben shouted. It was as good a sunny day as ever to lose a fortune. The big steer leaped out in the river and boys shouted to him. He swam across the river's current and soon the rest of the steers came filing in behind.

"Not too fast," Ben shouted, but over the bawling and horn rattling of eight hundred head he could have saved his commands. The cattle's calls in the river sounded afraid, but they swam in a fair order. One or two took courses of their own. Ben cringed watching them. He could only hope the dumb steer swimming in a circle didn't attract more. Another rode the current downstream until he high-centered astraddle a large tree and commenced complaining at the top of his lungs, caught by the current. Ben shook his head at the animal's dilemma. The best part was that most of the livestock were anxious as his cowboys to get to the other side and were headed up the bank, dripping wet, which made the climb slick, but the cattle were doing fine, save a half dozen idiots who'd wandered off on their own.

He could see Mark was tying ropes together and was still stripped down to his underwear, as were the rest of the crew. Mark coiled up the rope, put it over his shoulder, and began to swim toward the steer on the log. Wet as an otter he climbed out on the log, made a loop, and tossed it around the steer's horns after three tries.

The big critter wanted no part of it; he kept throwing his head at Mark but was unable to get any footing.

"Pull it!" Mark shouted, and Chip turned his horse with the rope on the horn. The hundred feet or so of lariat came flying out of the water, covered in moss, weeds, and sticks. Chip's pony dug in, and for a moment Ben wondered about the animal's strength. But he flipped the steer over and took off up the grade. Horns came up next out of the stained water and the half-drowned steer paddled with his head out and let out an angry bawl. Under again, this time he came up fighting with fury. Cowboys went to mount. Chip shucked his rope and headed up the hill.

Ben sent the gray off the bank and joined Digger on the drag. At last glimpse, the steer trailing lots of rope was headed for the main herd. Ben's gray needed a little encouragement and soon was swimming across. Ben clasped his hands on the horns and kicked his feet. The water's chill about took his breath, and he knew a fire would be in order.

The boys were roping cattle stuck in the mud and dragging them out. Most were too tired to fight; others came out on the prod and had to be avoided. Mark was dressing in his wet clothing when Ben reached the north shore.

"Good job," Ben said, riding past him. "Billy Jim, how many we lose?"

"My best count, two. We're going to ride downstream and check on them."

"All the hands here?"

"Yes, sir, cold as hell, but we're here."

"Someone build a fire. There's plenty of

wood. The rest of you try and find the missing ones."

"I got coffee up on top," Hap shouted.

"Forget building the fire; let's go have some coffee. Them two can wait."

They stood around swallowing hot coffee and shaking, while trying to get some heat out of the windswept cooking fire. Ben had never felt this cold in the rain.

Chip and Mark rode off to find the last two. Hap was drying out a pistol for one of the boys who had forgotten to put it in the wagon. The others were busy reassembling the herd before they scattered.

"We got lucky," Hap said, and Ben agreed.

"We're going to need lots of it. There's several more to cross."

"These boys are doing a good job," Hap said, still drying off the revolver.

"The best, under the circumstances." Ben watched them bringing in the strays. "I ain't too certain we didn't end up with better help than if we'd gotten all grown men."

Hap agreed, applying oil to the weapon's surface. "They give it their all."

He was on time by his schedule, he thought, looking across the rolling brown grassland of the Indian Nation that carried a hint of green. Thirty days north lay the Arkansas River and Kansas. Then they'd be within two weeks' drive of Abilene and Joe McCoy's shipping pens. His thoughts went to Jenny and the boys back home. If things went right he could be there by July. With a glance at the sky he asked the powers above for help and left camp to find the stray hunters.

He passed a mud-coated, exhausted steer obviously pulled from the Red's bottom. Through a copse of trees showing some early leafing, he rode into the open. Two cowboys were struggling to sled a bellowing steer on his side up a sharp bank.

"Wasn't no place else to do it," Mark shouted as he pressed his bay onward.

At last the critter was on the grassy surface. Chip dismounted, undid the lariats, and stepped back up while the muddy steer flailed his legs to get up.

"They don't always appreciate being saved," Chip said with a smile, and coiled up his rope.

"Boys, we did good today, but we've got plenty more crossings ahead."

Both of them nodded.

"No Sunday-school picnic, right?" Mark asked, twirling his lariat tail at the steer to get him going toward the herd.

"Right."

Five days north of the Red, Ben watched a bank of dark clouds gathering in the northwest. The temperature had turned hot and the dust boiled up from every hoof. By midafternoon they had reached the campsite and let the steers graze. By then the ominous wall towered higher in the sky, so Ben was forced to throw his head back to measure the height of them.

"Got your eye on her?" Hap asked, pouring coffee into Ben's tin cup.

"She won't get here till dark, but I figure when she comes it'll slam into us."

"Been going too smooth," Hap said. "Eight hundred crazy cattle and we've been going along like a milk-cow train."

"They aren't bad wild." Ben studied the dark curtain.

"Sure, but have they really been tested?" Hap asked. "I figure there's hail in that sucker. Lightning and sure enough hell to pay its due before morning. Too hot."

"I better start warning the boys."

Hap agreed and mopped his face on the kerchief from his hip pocket. "We ain't getting much sleep tonight. None of us."

By four o'clock, the rumble out of the storm's belly began to roll across the wide horizon. Ben considered that the herd was in a good bunch, but there was no telling what they'd do when the storm struck. It was as Hap had said, they'd never been tested. The entire trip the rains had fallen soft and the weather had been ideal. But the sky coming at them with lightning dancing over its face might be the challenge of the drive.

With everyone on horseback but Hap, they circled the herd, talking, singing, anything to distract the steers' attention from the freight train bearing down on them. The first breath of wind drew several head of longhorns to their feet. Their muzzles tested the wind, as if they wanted to know this new smell of cured grass and the freshness of the air.

Each man was in his yellow slicker on a fresh horse, riding, talking to the cattle. Filled with the anxiety of knowing the powder keg could blow at any moment, Ben pushed Roan along.

"Whoa, doggies," he repeated, waiting in anticipation for the first nearby crash. The suspense roiled his guts. He missed Jenny, wanted to hold her, hug her, and have her for his own. A glance to the west told him trouble would not be long in coming.

A triple blast of lightning and the resounding crash came as one. Steers jumped to their feet. Drops of rain pattered on Ben's slicker, then more blinding lightning and thunder. He looked across the herd and saw the fear in sixteen hundred eyes. He booted Roan and shouted louder as the first piece of hail struck his hat like a rock.

On cue, the herd bolted when the ice pellets started. Darkness was marked with repeated blinding strikes that danced over the ground. The drum of thousands of hooves, the plaintive bawling all mixed in with the roar of the hell they were in. There was nothing to do but try to head them off, to pray they weren't headed for one of the huge patches of prairie-dog villages that covered hundreds of acres in places, or a sheer drop-off, where Ben could visualize hundreds of carcasses piled up.

He spoke to urge on the hard-driving Roan, racing into the wall of darkness and being hammered by fist-sized hail. Maybe it was all foolish, this chase. He shouted at Roan as they moved beside the river of slick-wet steers running in fear. He needed to turn the leaders to make them circle. Hand on his hat, Ben felt more wind grabbing at him and wondered at the ear-shattering noise of a freight train if they were in a tornado.

Then it passed and he was beside the leader, who acted as if he was out of the will to run much more and circled to the right when he rode in close, waving his coiled rope at him.

In the west he saw a window of light and looked with relief to the east for the others. Mark and Chip were coming, Toledo and Miguel behind them. That left Digger, Dru, Lou. . . .

Their lathered, hard-breathing horses reined up. Both Mark and Chip shook their heads.

"You see that twister?" Chip asked.

Ben shook his head. "I heard it."

"Went north of us a little," Mark said. "Whew, we were lucky."

"Keep the herd here. I'll go look for the others."

"Who's missing?" Chip asked as he and Mark stood in the stirrups to look around for sight of them.

"Billy Jim, Digger, Dru, and the wrangler, Lou."

"There's Dru," Mark pointed out as the ex-soldier appeared on the far side.

"Mark, go tell him the plans and ask about the others. I'll ride back and look for them. You boys get them settled good; we'll start riding herd and get everyone fed some supper."

"Cool as this wind is, I'd say it was over," Chip offered, and they all agreed as the ragged edge of the end of the curtain began to drift away.

Ben worried more about three drovers he could not see. He loped Roan easily for the east. Standing in the stirrups, he stopped to talk to the two Mexicans.

"You seen any of the others?" he asked, taking a seat in the saddle.

"No, we were riding so hard," Miguel said.

"You all did good. Help keep the herd here and I'll go look for them."

He passed the tail end of the herd. Several head were scattered, and he smiled when at last he saw Digger and Billy Jim appear, driving the tailenders toward the herd.

"Any sign of Lou?"

"Not since before all hell broke loose, Mr. Ben," Digger offered, and the three searched around.

"We were getting up these to put in the herd, if you all ever caught them," Billy Jim said. "But we ain't seen Lou since it started."

"I'll ride back and see if I can find the boy. You keep gathering the strays."

"Yes, sir. Hope he ain't hurt none," Digger said.

"Me too." Ben took his leave and hurried on.

Where was the remuda? He'd not seen any horses in the herd. But had he looked closely? Searching for any sign from the high places, he soon spotted the wagon and rode over to talk to Hap.

"Get 'em stopped?" the cook asked, looking shaken.

"Yes. You seen Lou and the horses?"

"No, but I thought me and this wagon was going flying. It about turned the damn thing over. My washpan flew a hundred yards. Guess I was lucky to get it back. How's the rest?"

"Everyone's accounted for but the Chinaman."

"Reckon he was trampled?"

"No, him and the horses aren't in sight. Maybe I can find some sign of them. The horses weren't with the steers."

"I'll try to get some supper fixed," Hap said with a sigh.

"Do that. Part of them will be coming in when they get them settled out there."

"I can see one thing, Ben."

"What's that?"

"This cattle-driving business sure ain't for the faint of heart."

Ben agreed. Where was his celestial?

Chapter 18

The horse tracks were easy for Ben to follow once he cleared the cloven-hoofed ones of the herd. In the last of the day's light, with the sun firing the tops of the eastward-bound clouds, he short-loped the roan northward. The horses had broken to the north while the steers went west.

It would be too dark for him to even read track in thirty minutes. The moon wouldn't be up for an hour, but if Lou Song was after the remuda, maybe he had halted them already somewhere ahead and was trying to get back.

Ben kept pushing, the trampled grass and prints obvious, as some even cupped rain water. There was no way to ever get to Kansas without his horses. They couldn't handle the longhorns on foot. He'd heard stories of outfits who had lost their remuda to Indian raids and were forced to buy more horses to proceed.

Ben let Roan walk. The moon rose and he felt he was still on the track. Hours passed, and he hoped Chip and Mark had made some good decisions on the night-herding chores. Between them and Hap he felt satisfied the matters in camp were handled. How far had the horses run?

He paused on a high place and listened. A horse whined, then another. There was timber in the swale under him. Must be a stream down there. Soon the sharpness of woodsmoke came on the wind, and he wondered if Lou had built a fire.

Ben rode farther west, parallel to the valley, and saw the fire's light. Something made the hair on the back of his neck stand up and itch. No way that boy would have made such a blaze. He felt for the Colt on his hip. Satisfied the handgun was there, he booted Roan downhill. The cool wind drew goose bumps on his arms.

He could hear men's voices in the night, and saw the fire's glow dancing off a canvas shelter erected in the trees.

When he was close enough, he shouted, "Hello, the camp."

"Hello, yourself," someone answered. "Come on in."

Wary of everything around him, he recalled the words of advice from another drover who'd been to Baxter Springs, Kansas, the year before: *The Injuns can be bad up there, but the white men in the Nation are a real desperate lot.*

"Howdy stranger," a man wearing a stovepipe hat said, and came from the direction of the fire. "You're out kinda late, ain't ya?"

"I'm looking for my horse wrangler and horses."

"Guess you came to the wrong place for that. Me and the guys ain't seen 'em."

Ben stopped before entering the light of the fire. Right off, he didn't trust the man behind the beard facing him, holding on to the sides of his coat. His words didn't ring true.

"When the storm came, it spooked my horses. Lou Song is a short Chinese boy, about this high." He held out his hand to show the boy's height.

"Ain't seen no Chinaman. No horses but our own. We got some barley coffee; you want some?"

Ben felt undecided. He could see several men lounging around the fire. They looked tough enough. By himself he would have lots to handle if things got out of hand. If he thought they'd done anything to that boy he'd handle them. At the moment he thought the leader knew more than he was saying.

"Name's Graham. Udal Graham."

"McCollough's mine."

"Mr. McCollough, you must have a big herd of cattle." Graham led him like a Judas goat toward the firelight.

"Big enough," Ben said, keeping his wits about him.

"I mean if you have a herd of horses. You must have a bunch of cowboys."

"Several."

"Boys, this here is Mr. McCollough. He's lost his horses."

The men were seated on the ground, some in leather; others wore parts of uniforms. They laughed at Graham's words.

"Man loses his horses up here in the Nation, he might never find them," said a hard-looking man in his thirties wearing an eye patch, sitting cross-legged.

There were six men around the fire, plus Graham who was pouring some steaming coffee in a cup for Ben. "Here."

Two of them looked like breeds, besides One-eye and another with a thin, patchy blond beard, who Ben guessed was under twenty years old. The others were older, probably war vets.

"About my horses," Ben said, taking the cup in his left hand with a nod for thanks. "I intend to get them back."

His words drew more laughter that only grated him. Ben noticed Graham wore a small revolver in his waist band, probably a .30-caliber handgun. One-eye had a rifle leaned against a crate close by. White Beard dressed in buckskin with fringe wore a cross-draw holster with a large Walker Colt in the center of his stomach as he sat cross-legged in the fire's light.

"McCollough here says he lost a Chinaman," Graham said to the others. "I ain't never worried none about losing a damn chink. Have any of you boys?"

His question drew more laughter.

"That's fine," Ben said. "If anything's happened to my horse wrangler, there'll be hell to pay."

"Oh, Mr. McCollough, we ain't done nothing with your —"

Ben tossed the cup's hot contents in Graham's face. He dropped the cup as the man screamed, jerked him around by the lapel of his coat to use him as a shield, and drove the muzzle of his Navy .44 into the man's lower belly.

"Don't move or I'll blow daylight through his guts," he ordered.

"You'll never get away with this," Graham whined.

"I may not, but you'll be with me, 'cause

I'm writing your ticket to hell, mister!"

"Do as he says," Graham said over his shoulder.

Ben jerked the short gun out and stuck it in his waistband; then he roughly whirled Graham around to face them. "Now, what did you do with my boy?"

"Nothing."

"Your memory need a few knots on your head?" Ben said in his ear.

Hell broke loose. The breed on the left rolled sideways and Ben had to shove Graham aside to shoot at him. The second one drew a knife, and Ben shot One-eye in the side reaching for his rifle. In the gunsmoke and confusion, Graham screamed, and the breed's knife was sticking in his shoulder when Ben tried to survey the gang members in the fog of black powder.

"Don't none of you move!" he shouted, and his orders took hold. He edged over and took the rifle away from the groaning One-eye. The knife-tossing breed scowled at him, and the kid with his hands raised looked bug-eyed.

"Where's the boy at?" Ben demanded.

"Wagon." The kid swallowed. "I never did a thing to him."

Ben's gaze still on the crew, he edged over to look in the wagon. The sight of Lou's expression in the half light from the fire, though he was tied and gagged, made Ben feel much better.

He got out his jackknife with his left hand and cut Lou's hands free, and the boy quickly shed the kerchief over his mouth.

"I tell them you come shoot them asses off, Mr. Ben." Lou scampered out of the wagon and hit the ground. "They no listen me. Say they kill you. Ha, they not know Ben McCollough, huh?"

"They've been learning. Gather up their guns."

"Yes, sir, Mr. Ben. They think China boy him crazy, huh?" Lou jerked the pistol from the kid's holster. "Yes, you think me crazy?"

"No," warbled the kid.

"You get bullet in you?" he asked the wounded breed, while taking a knife from his scabbard. "Bad deal, maybe you die, huh?"

With the gang tied up, Ben considered what he should do next. Three needed medical treatment. They weren't his concern. The horses, Lou said, were, as he suspected, down the draw.

"Good, we'll keep the fire up tonight and take turns watching them. Come morning we'll get the horses and head back," Ben said.

"Plenty good."

"What did they have to eat?" Ben asked, looking around.

"Me fix us some food," Lou said. "Me damn hungry too."

"What about us?" the kid asked.

"When you get loose of those ropes you can fix your own damn food," Ben said, and winked at Lou, who beamed.

Between guarding and sleeping with one of his eyes half-open, Ben found little rest. The wounded ones moaned and groaned, but they didn't draw any sympathy from him or Lou. Before daylight, Lou made breakfast from their chuck box. Ben knew he'd be glad to get back to real coffee; the roasted barley was a piss-poor excuse for it.

"I'm leaving you a team of your stock to pull one wagon, but taking the rest. That should get you back to a doctor."

"What about . . . ?"

Ben nodded to the kid holding out his bound hands. "You'll just have to figure out how to untie yourself. I damn sure ain't."

With that he stepped up onto Roan and motioned to Lou that he was ready to leave. They gathered the horses and Ben cut out two feather-legged drafthorses that looked like a team. He drove them toward the camp, while Lou waved his lariat and pushed the horses up the hill.

Ben came back and helped the boy. When he looked up he could see in the golden light two riders on the hilltop.

"Got company, Lou," he shouted, and motioned to the ridge.

"Ah, more good men. Chip and Ward, they come too. Everyone worry about guy from China, huh?"

Ben laughed aloud. Yes, everyone worried about the guy from China. *We're moving, Jenny, headed north again. Thank God.*

Chapter 19

On the move again, the steers stretched out in a column of four and five. The rain helped settle the dust some. The sky was a clear azure blue, not a cloud in sight, and a cool north wind drew a chill on Ben's arms under his sleeves. He rode ahead to scout where they'd find water later that afternoon, and where they might find wood, a scarce commodity on the grassland, save along a few creeks and draws.

Dried buffalo or cow chips usually spoiled Hap's disposition. Ben noticed Hap had begun stockpiling any wood he could find. In fact, the supply wagon was plumb full of sticks and split pieces — what wasn't taken up by their food goods and bedrolls. Moving north every day, Ben considered, if the McCoy map were any account to scale, they were halfway to the Arkansas River. Meadowlarks sang to him, red-tailed hawks observed him, and bobwhite quail flushed at his approach.

He reined Roan up and studied the five

figures on the rise to the west. They were no doubt Indians, hatless, and they appeared to be armed. He'd seen a few villages, though he'd skirted the herd wide of them. These had to be Indians. No hats. Were they sizing him up? Were there others on horseback? His hand reached back and brought the Colt around where it would be handy on his hip.

There was no need to ride on. If they intended to stop or raid him, he wanted an answer. If war was about to be declared, he needed to know, to break out the rifles, get the boys ready. They might raid his outfit, but they'd not get the herd without paying a real price for it.

He rode up to what he considered a safe distance, perhaps an eighth of a mile, and stopped Roan. If they came whipping around the hill on their ponies he might not have enough lead time to escape; otherwise, he felt safe.

Soon two of them came off the hill toward him to palaver. One wore a buffalo head-dress; the other one wore a single eagle feather that rustled in the afternoon wind.

"Ho," Buffalo Head shouted.

"Ho," Ben shouted back.

"You bring cattle over our land?"

"You have any marks for your land or

fences?" Ben looked around as if searching for them.

"Great White Father give us this land."

"I'm moving north. Be out of here in a few days."

"You want to cross my land you pay me."

"I'd be glad to give you a couple crippled steers. They're only sore-footed. Let them at grass they'll be fine and fat in no time."

"Want ten good ones," Buffalo Head insisted.

"Wanting and getting are two different things. I can't pay that many." Ben shook his head. No way.

"You pay or you no go by here."

"Where's your village?" Ben asked.

"My village is that way." Buffalo Head pointed northwesterly. "You bring ten head my village."

"Well, I ain't paying no ten head. I might give you two."

"Me make war." He pointed at Ben and shook his head in rage.

"You want to go see spirit in the sky?"

"Huh?" Buffalo Head frowned at Ben, then at the buck with him.

"Well, you get in my way you might go there — real quick-like."

Ben had enough of the belligerent devil and told him he would see him. He turned

Roan and rode off before Buffalo Head could say anything else to make him mad.

That afternoon, Ben and Mark cut out two footsore oxen and headed them toward the village. The animals went slowly, but they were easy to herd, unable to run back to the rest. They came over the last ridge, and the smoke of cooking fires reached Ben's nose.

"Lodges, huh?" Mark asked.

"Lodges, they ain't the tepee kind."

"Ain't got any ponies either," Ben said, observing things.

"Where did they go? Men ride them away?"

"Don't know, Mark. I ain't heard any dogs either."

"Where would they be?"

"Ate them, if they're as hungry as they look." Ben nodded to the thin-faced woman standing by her lodge doorway wrapped in a tattered blanket.

"Oh, that's horrible." Mark made a face.

"Ate their horse herd to get by on." Ben cranked his head around when the two steers stopped.

An old man came out of a lodge with a red-and-blue blanket wrapped around him. His thin white hair was in braids.

"Chief, you can eat these two *wahoos*."

"Eat two." The old man bobbed his head in agreement. "You get down. You eat too. My people plenty glad you come."

"One with buffalo head on?" Ben made signs like he wore the headdress.

"Black Bull?"

"I don't know his name. But he threatened me. I was mad. I can see that your people need food."

"No buffalo here," the old man said, holding his hands out to mean anywhere around him. "Shoot him with guns till he run away. Indians kill with arrows, not scare buffalo."

"Tell Black Bull, I'll bring more wahoos."

"You good man." Then he said something guttural and women began to appear, armed with butcher knives.

In seconds the steers laid bleeding on the ground, their throats cut. The army of females young and old began to skin and dissect the still-trembling cattle. Mark made a face at Ben, who shook his head to refrain him from saying anything.

A stout Indian woman worked deftly, with her blade slicing open the belly of the first one and exposing the purple and pink viscera. She sliced away the brownish liver and then held it up in one hand while her assistant poured the gall juices over it. She

238

stepped over and offered it to Ben.

When he hesitated, she insisted. "You eat some. Make you better man."

He took the liver and her knife, bit off a hunk, sliced the rest free close to his face.

"Him too," she ordered, motioning to Mark.

His mouth full of the hot, bitter liver, Ben nodded for Mark to continue. Each chew only increased the strong flavors. Ben hoped it did him as much good as she thought it would, as the fumes even burned his nose.

Poor Mark, he thought, but the youth followed his lead; then he handed the knife and liver back to her. The squaw boldly slapped him on the leg and shouted something that made the rest of the butchers laugh. Ben felt sure she had mentioned that it would improve Mark's virility.

Ben reined the roan around and nodded to the old chief. "Tomorrow I will bring you four more."

"You are brother to my people," the man said, and they left the camp.

Away from their camp, Mark rinsed his mouth out with water from his canteen and spit it away. "Oh, that was bad."

Ben reached back and found the bottle of whiskey in his saddlebags. He handed the pint across to Mark. "Try a little of this."

"Whew, anything's better than raw liver. Damn! And why pour all that bitter gall on it?"

"I'm not Indian; can't say."

"You see that one woman eating that piece of gut and squeezing the crap out the other end?"

"That's hunger."

"Yeah, worse than I ever saw. What will they do for food?" Mark asked, looking back.

"I don't know."

"Bothered you, didn't it, Ben?"

"Would have bothered anyone. No one deserves to starve."

"I agree." Mark shook his head and his shoulders quaked in revulsion.

"Boy, that liver was the worst thing I ever had in my mouth."

"Let's lope," Ben said after he put the whiskey away.

In camp later, Ben squatted on his heels and sipped Hap's coffee. He'd finished telling him what they'd found in the Indians' camp.

"That Mark's getting him a hell of a education this summer," Hap said. "Been drug off to a Mexican cathouse by Miguel, shot some Mexican bandits, swam the Red

River, been in a stampede and a tornado, and now ate raw liver with an Indian squaw. His poor maw would die if she knew all that's happened in his sixteenth summer."

"How old were you?" Ben asked, letting the coffee's steam soften the beard stubble around his mouth.

"I was fourteen when I shot my first man. He was a Comanche climbing in the window of our ranch house. I blew his head half-off with that shotgun — my knees were shaking so bad they were clattering."

"When did the rest happen?"

"I met me the finest little *señorita* in San Antonio that summer. My, my, she was sweet. I can still recall looking at her without any clothes on and them knees of mine liked to caved in. Whew-ha."

"Time you were sixteen?"

"I was a Texas Ranger, fighting Injuns, drinking raw whiskey, and taking on all the girls in the cantina when I came in."

"So what's so bad about what he's done?"

Hap looked off at the fiery sunset that filled the western sky. He shook his head. "Just ought to be different. He's got schooling; I never had any. You told me if you went to school you was supposed to be more civilized."

"It ain't always that way."

"How old were you when you discovered there's a difference in boys and girls?"

"Fifteen, I reckon. On a wagon train, when my family was coming to Texas. There was girl named Posey. Seventeen. She asked me if I ever did it. I told her lots of times. She called me a liar. Afterward, she said maybe I wasn't a liar." Ben shook his head, amused at the recollection. "She married Arthur Morton when the train got to Austin."

"Break your heart?"

"I think so — did for the moment, anyway."

"Why haven't you ever married?" Hap brought the pot over to refill Ben's coffee cup.

"I've had some bad luck with women I intended to marry. Guess why I worry about Jenny from time to time."

"Well, Ben, you and her deserve each other. She's a fine lady. Damn, if you'd sent me over there with one more deer I'd have married her myself. It's going to work out for you two, and we keep going, you'll be back and married before the summer's over."

"I hope so," Ben said, with her on his mind.

Chapter 20

They crossed the Washita without a problem or the loss of a single head of steer. Scouting ahead, Ben met a small company of soldiers. The shavetail lieutenant acted cordial enough that Ben paused to visit with him.

"Lots of you Texans coming up here with herds," the lieutenant — who introduced himself as Barry Clements — said as they sat their horses.

"All looking for markets for our cattle."

"Been some problems up near Baxter Springs with cattlemen and locals, I heard."

Ben nodded. "Reason that I'm this far west. Joe McCoy's supposed to have a shipping yard ready at a place called Abilene. That's west of the Kansas deadline for Texas cattle."

"All these cattle I've been seeing going past here, the price may be way down."

"That would be my luck. Indians are peaceful, I guess."

"Most of them."

"Most of them are starving, I've seen."

"Not my job to feed them. I agree they don't have much to eat. The buffalo are all west of here."

Ben nodded. "I better get to moving. Most of these creeks have rock bottom north of here?"

"Yeah, you've crossed the boggy ones. I ain't never crossed the Arkansas, though."

"It's still a ways north?"

"A good ways."

"Thanks," Ben said, then threw him a salute and set the gray to a short lope. He needed a place to stop for the night. Besides, it looked like more rain was coming. It beat having a drought, but in the mud, cattle got hard to drive, and the way was hard for Hap, his wagon, and the mules.

In midafternoon he shot a fat deer, bled it, and hung it in a cottonwood beside a stream big enough to water the herd. Then he started back to find Hap. Rain arrived before he found the wagon, and he pointed out the way. Hap in his slicker on the seat looked exasperated, but simply grumbled at him.

"There's a deer hanging in a cottonwood."

"I'll find it." Then, with a shout at his ear-flicking mules, he went on.

"Hap not in good mood," Lou said when

Ben stopped to talk to him.

"Reckon he's sitting on a cactus pad?"

"Maybe so. Him mad since sun came up."

"Guess he'll have to get glad by himself." Ben shook his head as the rain came off the brim of his hat. "How's the horses doing?"

"Two crippled, but they get better. Must pull muscle in leg getting steer out of mud."

"Couple need some salve. They've got saddle sores."

"Oh, me treat them. Every night we get to camp."

"Good, we need them all well. It'd still be a ways to walk to Kansas."

"We get there, I shout, have fireworks, big time, huh, Mr. Ben?"

"All that and more." Ben smiled and turned the gray into the light rain. Best he go find the swing riders, Mark and Chip. It would be a long afternoon at this rate to make camp.

Cattle grazing at last, the riders not on guard were huddled under Hap's canvas fly to escape the downpour.

"Be to the Arkansas River in a week?" Chip asked.

"I think so." Ben nodded, listening to the pitter-pat on the cloth ceiling.

"How wide you reckon it is?"

"Can't say. But we're upstream some from where others been crossing it in years past. If the snowmelt in the West hasn't reached this far yet, it shouldn't be too hard to ford."

Chip nodded like he was satisfied. Ben knew the river crossings bothered Dru worse than the boys. The older man grew more silent the farther they went. He mentioned once to Ben that he should never have come. When Ben quizzed him on why, he shrugged. "Cattle driving ain't my thing."

Ben imagined that when Dru collected his hundred dollars' salary he'd head straight for some bar and drink until the money was gone. Plenty of soldiers came home from the war and did the same thing — fell in the bottle.

"Mr. Ben?"

He turned and nodded to Billy Jim. "What's that?"

"Be lots of Yankees in Kansas?"

"I guess. But the war's over."

"I sure hope so."

"We all need to get on with our lives and forget it."

"My paw won't; he hates them. I just hope I can recognize them when I see them so I can avoid them."

Ben shook his head in amusement. "Billy Jim, they look just like the rest of us."

"Hell, how'll I know 'em?"

"When they open their mouth to talk," Chip said, and everyone laughed.

Hap broke up the party by serving fried apple pies to everyone. The surprise treat mellowed out the entire crew; even Dru acted pleased.

"Thought you was mad about something?" Ben asked when they were to the side. The sweetness of each bite flooded his mouth with saliva.

"I was mad. Can't remember why now. Must not have been important, 'cause after me and Lou got the deer butchered in the rain, I figured we all needed some cheering up."

Ben held up the half-eaten pie. "Good idea."

The deep fork of the Canadian furnished a rock bottom and they went through it with ease, then the Salt Fork of the Arkansas. But the land beyond that crossing was slashed with deep ravines and no timber. Until they crossed Grapevine Creek, the grazing was slim, too. But the thick grass on the north side filled the steers up quickly. Ben decided to scout the Arkansas, so he told the boys they'd rest there with the good water and wood, and graze the herd for two days.

Mark rode with him, and they hurried across the prairie. Neither man said much from the bluff looking at the wide river they must conquer: six hundred yards across, hemmed in by steep bluffs. There was no bottom land to hold the herd, and wherever they went in, they would need a route to get out also.

They found some places where others had gone over. Stripped down to underwear they went across on horseback, finding that the water was deep enough to force their horses to swim for only a hundred yards. The current worried Ben some. On the far shore they discovered some logs that others must have used to keep their wagons afloat.

"We can snake them back, we can use them to float Hap's rig," Ben said.

"We'll have to move him over first," Mark said, more as a statement than a question.

"I think so. Be easier on the mules. All those wet steers coming out of the river would make this hillside slick for the mules' footing."

"We get Hap and the horses across, then bring up the steers."

Ben agreed, and they rode up to the top of the hill. Northward the hills were taller, but covered in rich-looking grass. The only good thing on Ben's mental list: Kansas wasn't far.

They rode back, took the logs with them on lariats, forded the river, and, after drying some in the sun, dressed and headed back for the herd. They arrived in late afternoon.

"How wide is it?" Billy Jim asked.

"Over a quarter mile," Mark said.

"But there's only a short distance the horses have to swim," Ben added.

"Short? Like how far?"

"It'll be a damn sight easier to cross than the Red. There's current, but I think we can make it smooth enough," Ben said.

"Billy Jim, we're all going to make it," Mark said with finality.

"Well, okay."

The next day, Billy Jim, Chip, Mark, and Ben went back to drag more logs to the south bank. The floats for the wagon were drawn back and stacked up, ready to lash onto Hap's rig.

"Mark, you and Chip will each have long ropes tied to the front chain. You two will go ahead and be close to the bank when the mules hit the water deep enough that they have to swim. With both of you using your horses to pull them, they should get over here safe and sound."

Chip nodded, impressed. "I worried about the Comanche donkeys and how they'd do out there. That'll solve that problem."

"Then we'll go back, get the herd, and bring them over."

"Your map show any more rivers?" Billy Jim asked, standing around in the bright sunshine with the others in their wet underwear.

"This is the biggest one," Ben promised.

"I may turn out to be a fish before we get there," Billy Jim said, and started to dress.

"Least you had two baths today," Chip said. "You won't smell so bad that way."

Everyone laughed, and Billy Jim shook his head in disapproval.

They ate before daylight the next morning, and Hap drove the wagon to the river. Ben left the two Mexican boys with the herd and the rest went along to help. Logs were tied tight to each side in bundles. Hap had the look of man at a funeral when Ben clapped him on the shoulder.

"How many times we do this in the war?"

"Yeah, but those were the army's wagons, not mine," Hap said, and checked a knot on the top log.

Ben sent the boys in the lead with their tow ropes. When the boys reached the point in the stream where their ropes were tight, Hap laid the reins to the mules. They went off into the Arkansas on their tiptoes. Used to crossing, they didn't do badly, though there was some hesitation and more cuss words when they hit the part where that horse had to swim. The boys made the bank with their wet ponies digging in, and to Ben's relief the mules soon found footing and a hurrah went up. The wagon was across.

The logs undone, Hap took his mules up the grade. Lou came off the bluff through the wide draw with the horse herd and they headed straight for the bank.

"Looks good, Ben," Mark said as the wrangler went up the far hill with the remuda and waved to them.

"Now get eight hundred and forty more across, plus us, and we're headed for Abilene," Ben said.

It was ten a.m., according to the sun, when Mark and Chip choused the black steer, Stonewall Jackson, in the murky brown water. The faraway sandstone bluffs towering above the river looked even farther away to Ben than when they first swam their horses across two days earlier. The file of steers coming by fours and fives looked orderly enough from his position. A few acted like fools and leaped out in the shallow water like they were going off a bluff. Their incisive bawling picked up. Miguel and Toledo moved out to hold the cattle in a line. He noticed that Billy Jim and Dru were working opposite sides and keeping the cattle in a steady stream. Back at the rear, Digger brought the stragglers.

It was as orderly as any army's movement, Ben decided over the noise of the steers splashing and cowboys shouting commands. He pushed the gray off the hillside. Digger would need some help; the last ones always were reluctant to take to water.

He was making the gray work back and forth, to keep the end of the line moving, when he heard Billy Jim shout, "Dru's fell off his horse!"

Digger jerked his pony around and frowned. There was no time for explanations; Ben wheeled the gray to take to the hillside and pass the herd. He pushed the gelding hard through the brush and emerged on the river's edge. From his vantage point, he could see Billy Jim swimming his horse through the cattle to get to Dru. A riderless horse was headed for the bank a hundred yards down the Arkansas.

Ben and the gray plunged into the river. "No, Billy, let me." The gray charged into the stream, stepped off into a hole, and began to swim. The youth never heard him above the bawling cattle — Ben still could not see Dru. Then he spotted a familiar hat floating away downstream. He clung to the saddle horn as the big horse swam. His boots were full, and the cold water saturated his clothing.

Where was Dru? It made no sense. Why didn't he surface?

"Bill! Head for the shore," he shouted, and the wild-eyed youth on his circling horse looked at him like he'd said the impossible.

"But Ben —"

"I know, but your horse ain't a fish. You'll wear him down. Head for the shore. Now!"

"What about Dru?"

Ben raised himself as high as he could above the dog-paddling gray and saw no sign of the man, only the wide, rippled brown surface. He shook his head and waved Billy away. "Go on; we've done all we can."

Mark had ridden down the bank to help them. Ben saw him standing on his saddle, hands cupped against the glare, looking, when he reached the water's edge.

"I'm sorry, Ben. I just wanted to save him." Billy Jim looked depressed, standing in his sodden one-piece underwear.

"You did the right thing."

"He never came up. He fell off and never came up," Billy said in disbelief.

Ben clapped him on the shoulders. "Not anyone's fault. He had the best horse to cross on. We told him how."

"Why did he rein him up?"

"No telling. Maybe he got scared."

Ben looked over the last of the herd coming out of the cold water and shaking a spray. The black cowboy's sleek ebony skin shone in the sun — he owned no underwear. Digger waved his rope and slapped cattle with his pooper on the end. Ben could regret not undressing beforehand as he poured water out of his boot, expecting a fish. He'd dry — Dru wouldn't.

Chapter 21

They held services for Dru, though they searched for a day and no body was recovered. It was like the Arkansas swallowed him, some of the boys said.

In the early morning they bowed their heads, and Ben read Psalms from the tattered Bible he'd carried through the war. Hap had carved a cross out of red cedar for Dru and planted it to the side of the crossing.

"Boys, Dru wasn't happy in this world. Perhaps God called him to Him. May he rest in peace, amen."

"Amen," came the chorus.

"We're two weeks or so from Abilene, boys. We'll take our time; these steers still look slick to me despite the drive. Maybe we can sell them and get home before summer's over."

Nodding their heads, their faces solemn, they set out.

Ben marked them off on his map each day: Spring Creek. Prairie Creek, Rock, and

Walnut. He met a small detachment from Fort Wichita on his scout.

"How many cattle you all got in Texas, anyway?" the old sergeant asked with a shake of his bald head as he replaced his cap.

"Plenty," Ben said.

"I'd say so. Have any Injun trouble in the Nation?"

"Only one bunch, and they were starving."

"Be more of them hungry than that. We ain't seen a buffalo in three days."

Ben agreed.

"Well, if you Rebs stay on this furrow you'll make it to the shipping pens."

"I expected to run into an Indian trader, half-Cherokee called Chisholm," Ben said. "Several boys been up the trail before talked about him being along in here."

"Back on the Arkansas Fork and west a little was his trading post. John died last winter from eating bad bear grease. Buried him down on the Canadian."

"Guess I won't meet him then in this world."

"No, you won't. He was a good man," the sergeant said. "He was at lots of peace conferences. He could talk I don't know how many languages. But he sure was hospitable."

"That's what I heard."

"You figuring on making this cow driving your living now?" the sarge asked, shifting in the McClelland saddle.

Ben shook his head. "I get these sold I'll be happy to stay home."

"Take care, Reb."

"You too."

They parted, men who might have sighted rifles at each other only a few years before. Both of them were old enough and smart enough to know the war was over. A hundred yards farther on, Ben flushed a covey of quail from the stirrup-high grass. McCoy's man had cut the furrow and mounded the sod in piles. The route was as well marked as turnpikes in the East. Their effort must have taken several ox teams to ever churn up this thick a matt of grass and roots. Probably they'd had one of those new steel plows someone named Deere had recently patented.

Three men rode a ridge to Ben's right. He was unsure how long they'd been out there. They wore cowboy hats. Ben realized they'd shadowed him for close to an hour. Anyone who would do that had to be up to something, Ben decided. Sizing him up. He reached the bottoms of Cottonwood Creek, where he intended to camp for the night, and reined Roan into a copse of trees.

He eased the Spencer out and waited, sitting on horseback. Birds chirped in the trees; robins darted about; Roan stomped a hoof at an occasional fly. The wind began to pick up in the cottonwoods. A fish flopped in the creek. There was no sign of the riders; Ben dismounted and searched for any sign of them from cover. Nothing.

Perhaps he was getting edgy. After he tied the flag up for Hap, he shoved the rifle into the scabbard, checked his cinch, and headed back for the herd in a short lope. He looked over his shoulder a lot and saw nothing out of place, but still, his gut instinct said to watch carefully. No one wanted to steal a herd in Texas, but a week's drive away from a place to sell them wouldn't be a bad deal.

"Hap, keep that shotgun close. Have Lou tie the horses on a picket line, and break out the Spencers." He reined up in camp.

"You see trouble today?"

"Three white men acted real interested in my business near the creek where I left the marker for you."

Hap rubbed his whiskered mouth on the side of his fist. "Damn, I thought we were going to get there unscathed, Ben."

"I may only be jumpy, but they acted like

258

they were up to no good."

"We'll be ready."

"Good, don't take any chances."

"I won't. You see that smoke in the west?"

Ben nodded. He'd seen the black smoke at a good distance from them so far. "Prairie fire. There will be more of them, if it doesn't rain."

"Hell, I was halfway enjoying being dry."

Both men laughed. And Ben rode on to talk to the boys with the herd.

Sunset scorched the western skies. Bobwhites whistled, and even a whippoorwill began his calling. The camp bristled with rifles. Everyone listened. Digger was busy setting limb lines to catch catfish. His contributions made their meals more varied, and the others even helped him fillet them. The day's heat evaporated.

Miguel put his finger to his lip, took up his Spencer, and headed from camp, moving low for the trees beyond the fire's light. Chip indicated that he heard something, and Ben took up a rifle and placed it over his lap.

"Hello, the camp."

Ben nodded to the crew. "Hello, yourself. Door's open."

"Guess them steers are yours?" a man in a suit said. Three men in cowboy gear came behind him.

"Name's Radamacher. My boys here and I wanted to come by and warn you."

Ben nodded, not offering to get up nor shake the man's hand.

Radamacher wore a brown suit and a derby hat — no ordinary drover. He looked more like a businessman than anything else, yet Ben didn't trust his shifty eyes sizing everything up as he stood, arms folded, in the reddish-orange fire light.

"Good. Being from so far away we could stand some warning," Ben said.

"Well, this cattle market has fallen apart," Radamacher said, and his men nodded like the world had ended. "There's been runs on the banks back east, and an army of unemployed and veterans have marched on Washington. Can I show you the article?" He reached into his coat and drew out a folded newspaper.

Ben accepted it and unfolded the Saint Louis *Chronicle*. Headlines said what the man spoke about. The date of issue was Sunday, March 21, 1868. Ben shook his head ruefully. "Looks bad. What are you doing?"

"Since cattle prices are so low and many

herds are gathered around up here, I came out to offer to buy your herd. I know you've got lots of expenses and no doubt owe money. I have some markets in the Midwest, but they'll only take fifty head a week, and at a much reduced price."

"Go on," Ben said.

"I can offer you four dollars a head in gold coin for your herd."

"That sure isn't much." Ben studied the man, who had dropped to squat, balancing on his dapper shoes. "Let me think on that, Mr. Radamacher."

"Well, there are several herds already up here I can buy, but you looked like an honest man, so I really felt I should offer you this first."

"I see."

Ben set the rifle aside and rose to his feet. The buyer threw his head back and stood. "You will find no markets in Abilene, sir. My offer can't hold for very long. I assure you, sir, that you will rue the day you didn't accept my generous offer."

"Sure, I will. Thanks for coming by." Ben motioned to the toughs still in the shadows. "I'll take my chances in Abilene, and anyone tries to take this herd can expect a bellyful of lead."

"I'm a reputable cattle buyer,"

Radamacher said, as if offended by his words.

"Still, you heard me. Don't mess with me or my hands."

"Well, I can see that you're too hard-headed to accept a genuine offer. I feel sorry for you when you have to winter your stock up here and take less next year than I offered for them. Like that newspaper said, the U.S. economy is in a shambles."

Ben waved him off and the four men left.

"What made you not do business with him?" Mark asked, looking off in the darkness after them. "Besides they were fish eyes."

"The twenty-first of March wasn't on a Sunday this year."

"Huh?" Billy Jim asked.

"That Saint Louis newspaper I'd never heard of, and I've never heard of any of them was dated Sunday, March twenty-first."

"How do you figure that, Ben?"

"It was a phony newspaper printed to show me how bad the market was so I'd panic and sell to him."

"How did they do that?" Digger asked.

Ben shook his head. "They can do all sorts of things, including print counterfeit money. Wouldn't be no problem to print a dummy newspaper."

Billy Jim shook his head in disbelief. "Guess that's why you're the boss."

Ben nodded and went off to relieve himself. He hoped those men heeded his warning. And the whole thing was a hoax. The night wind swept over his bearded face. *Jenny, I'll be headed home soon, God willing.*

Chapter 22

Abilene, aside from the wooden framework of a two-story building going up, hardly impressed Ben when he rode in town wearing his new leather shirt under his rain gear. He saw dirt-roofed cabins, several freighter wagons, and oxen teams in the street. There were unballasted railroad tracks, freshly built shipping pens, and new Fairbanks ten-ton scales — but not much signs of any other progress as the steady rain drilled down on his slicker.

He dropped off the gray and hitched him before a place marked *Fine Foods.* He beat the water off his hat on the leaky porch and pushed inside.

A tall man with a full mustache, wearing a suit and Ben guessed about thirty years old nodded to him. "You must have just arrived?"

"Ben McCollough, Kerr Mac County, Texas."

"Joe McCoy. Pleased to meet you, Ben."

"Well, Colonel, you're the reason I am

here. Your man Blair was down in Texas last fall and told me about this place. Followed his map, in fact."

"Have any trouble?"

Ben shook his head. "One thing worried me: There's rumors that the market is gone."

McCoy clapped him on the shoulder. "Those dirty buggers meet you down south and said sell to them? Market's gone?"

"Even had a newspaper said so."

McCoy narrowed his eyes and looked hard at Ben. "You didn't believe them?"

"No."

"Good. Fat steers sold for forty dollars today. How many of them do you have?"

"Four hundred. Plus four hundred two-year-olds in good flesh."

"The twos should get you twenty-two if they're good ones."

"Your man last fall said they needed steers, not cows, not heifers. I brought steers."

"Smart man. I think some drovers left home with all they had on the place and then they wonder why they can't get them sold."

"You eaten?" Ben asked.

"Yes, but help yourself, Ben. I'll be talking to you. In fact, come by afterward and see Mr. Kane; he may want to look at your cattle."

"Scales?"

"Yes. My new offices aren't built yet. Good to meet you, and glad you didn't believe those scoundrels."

"So am I," Ben said. McCoy would never know how hard Radamacher's first words had kicked him in the chest. All that way for nothing, he had feared. A rascal was all he was.

An hour later he talked to Orlon Kane in McCoy's office, and the men discussed cattle prices.

"This rain lets up, I'll be out where you're holding your herd. In the morning Ralston Farnam may be with me. He needs some feeder cattle for some Illinois farmers that the twos might fit."

Ben shook his hand and left for camp. It was the fifteenth of April and he might already have his herd sold. If he could be that lucky. Going back to camp, he understood what McCoy meant about mixed herds. There were cattle grazing in all directions — cows, calves, even, along with yearlings and old castrated bulls. They must have figured the market was so good that they could sell anything.

That was the reason his old buyer in

Mexico had complained so about Ben's demand for steers only. It was a lot easier to grab anything and rustle it. He listened to a meadowlark's shrill five-note call. Clouds were breaking up; the morning might bring one of the greatest days in his life.

"What're we doing?" Chip asked when he dismounted.

"Cross your fingers, and Toledo, burn a candle in the church. Buyers are coming in the morning to look at them. Both sets."

"Whew," Chip said, and the others nodded approval.

"What's town like?" Billy Jim asked.

"Dirt-floored saloons. It's a tough-looking place, and fat, ugly women's all I saw you'd be interested in."

"Why, I thought Abilene was a big city."

"A grubby hole so far. They're building on it."

"Ugly fat women?" Chip asked, taken aback.

"They may be hiding all the pretty ones, but the ones I saw you could smell across the street."

Mark laughed. "Guess we'll have to go back to Mexico, Billy Jim."

"He ain't forgot her either," Chip added.

"Least she wasn't fat, ugly, and smelled bad," Billy Jim said.

"I take you back," Miguel said.

"Boys, I bought a bottle of whiskey to celebrate. Get your cups. In a few days you can go in and see the Sodom and Gomorrah of the plains."

Hap laughed and shoved a cup at him. "I'll be ready. You selling the horses too?"

"Never thought about it. They might be worth more here than back at home. We could cut out what we need to ride home on and sell the rest. How about your mules?"

"We'd have to sell the wagon."

"You ain't married to it, are you?"

"Lord, no, I'd love for someone else to have them biting, kicking flea bags."

"We'd have to go home with some pack-horses."

"Greasy-sack outfit, huh?" Hap raised his whiskey to the others. "Here's to Texas, where us Rebs belong."

Ben looked up and saw Toledo riding in hard.

"*Señor* Ben, those men came the other night are out by the herd."

"Radamacher?"

"*Sí.* I counted several more too."

"Get the rifles, Hap. Catch your horses, boys."

In minutes they were armed, mounted, and hurrying for the herd. When they came within sight of them, Toledo pointed to the men wearing flour-sack masks. They were firing pistols in the air to spook the cattle. Ben rose up in the stirrups on the rocking gait of the gray, squeezed his knees to the fenders, and fired the Spencer. He levered in another cartridge, and then another. The rustlers veered off, but they had the cattle on the run.

"Mark, you take some hands and get the herd back. Chip, you come with me. We're going to end this bunch's stealing once and for all."

He and the ex-ranger pushed hard. The rustlers disappeared over the ridge and out of sight toward the Smoky Hill river country. Tracks were plain in the mud, and in a few hours they led Ben and Chip to a good-sized soddy in the river bottom under some large walnut trees.

A dozen or so spent, lathered horses stood around, hip-shot, still saddled. Ben and Chip, with several tubes of cartridges and their rifles, used stealth to get close in.

"What're we going to do next?" Chip asked, on his belly and parting the tall grass to better see the structure.

"Someone's coming outside," Ben said under his breath, taking aim.

Chip nodded.

"Nobody's out here," the rustler shouted back toward the house.

"Put your hands up," Ben ordered, using an uprooted cottonwood tree for cover.

The outlaw went for his pistol. The black smoke from the revolver fringed his face as the .50-caliber rifle bullet struck his chest and threw him backward six feet and onto his back.

"You got one chance," Ben shouted. "Come out unarmed. Hands in the air!" His order echoed back. There was no sign of anyone obeying him.

A figure showed himself with a handgun. Chip's Spencer barked and the shooter screamed, falling back inside. Then from the two windows a host of pistol shots answered him.

Ben fired into the window on the left, with a tinkle of glass and the cries of a man hit. Chip's barrage did the same on the right one. Another desperate outlaw charged out the door with a six-gun in each hand — he died a few steps from the opening, facedown in the dirt.

"How many are left?" Chip asked.

"Can't be many." Ben rolled over and saw Mark and Billy Jim coming down the slope.

"Guess they got the herd slowed down,"

Chip said, and turned back.

"I didn't figure they'd run far," Ben said, turning his attention back on the soddy.

"Herd's fine," Mark said, taking a place beside them. "They didn't run anywhere."

"Good. Those buzzards are inside, but they may be carving their way out the back. Chip, you and Billy Jim want to head around there?"

"Sure," Chip said, and, running in a crouch with Billy on his heels, he skirted the house.

In minutes there were more rifle shots. Ben rose. "Time to close in."

The two raced to the side of the soddy. Gunsmoke boiled out the door as Ben rested his shoulder against the thick, matted roots that made the block wall. Wounded men moaned. He drew a deep breath, set down the rifle, and took out his Colt.

"Give up or get ready to die!"

"We give up. Coming out."

Ben gave an exhale of relief. "Hands high, and get out here."

"We've got the back, Ben," Chip shouted.

Mark moved in and disarmed them as they filed out, hands high, grumbling, some of them bloody from wounds.

"Two in here are dead," Chip said, and

271

he came out coughing on the thick smoke.

Billy Jim followed him out, equally choking on gunsmoke. "Bad in there. Whew."

"Mark, gather ropes and horses."

"I'll help," Billy Jim said.

Chip lined the four outlaws against the wall of the house.

"What're you going to do with us?" the hard-faced older one asked.

"Why, hang you, of course," Ben said.

"Figured so," the outlaw said.

Despite the rustlers' angry protests, Ben and his men tied their hands behind their backs, mounted them on horseback, dropped nooses over some thick limbs of the cottonwoods breaking their dormancy with a shower of new green leaves.

Each outlaw was in a saddle; only the wind in the treetops and the sniffling of one of the rustlers could be heard. Ben swung his coil of lariat and busted the older one's horse on the butt and then three others followed suit. The rustlers danced their final set and one of them released his bowels.

Ben never looked back; he headed for the gray. Justice was served. Except Radamacher. He'd make him pay too, before it was all over.

Out of breath, Billy Jim caught up with him. "Less and less like a picnic," he said, and caught his horse.

Ben agreed.

Chapter 23

The two buyers came in a buckboard. They drove out to a high point with Ben, Chip, and Mark. The multicolored longhorns spread across the brown-grass prairie occasionally lifted a head out of curiosity to look in their direction.

"How many culls?" Kane asked.

Ben nodded at Mark to speak.

"Four hundred and six good steers in the big ones. Twenty more are not as good. They aren't bad, but might limp some."

"I don't need anything but good steers," Kane said.

"Four hundred six, then, that we can deliver, sir."

"I'd give thirty-five dollars apiece for them."

Ben stood looking off to the south. He hadn't ridden across the face of the earth to be robbed. He shook his head. "I'd take forty-two and not check with anyone."

"Whew," Kane said, and made an angry face at him.

Ben slapped his chaps with the ends of the reins. "Mr. Farnam, are you interested in the two-year-olds?"

"Yes, you have how many head?" the thinner man asked, taking off his fancy hat and scratching the nearly bald crown of his head.

"We can deliver four hundred ten head," Mark said to Ben's nod of approval.

"They all as uniform as I see?"

"Here, take Roan and ride through them," Ben offered. "These cattle aren't crazy."

"I noticed. Those corn farmers hate wild cattle."

Ben held out the reins for the man, who refused with a head shake.

"I'd bid twenty-three dollars apiece on a close cull."

"Make it twenty-five and I'll throw in the ten," Ben said. No need to be greedy. That was ten thousand. He could turn his back on the rest and ride home a richer man than he expected. Kane wasn't through either.

The bays hitched to the buckboard snorted in the grass and shifted their weight, making the harness jingle. A steer bawled, and the cry was taken up by the strong south wind that whipped the grass tops like ocean waves.

"I think you're probably the best cattleman I've dealt with," Ralston said. "No heifers in there?"

"Not that's ours," Ben said.

"We haven't seen one," Chip said, and grinned. "We've looked them over a lot."

Mark chuckled to himself and nodded. "We've sure seen them all."

"How many did you lose?" Kane asked.

"Five," Mark said, "not counting some we gave the Indians and ate ourselves."

"You were lucky," Kane said.

"Start delivering in two days," Ralston said to Ben. "Twenty-five apiece for four hundred, and ten extras. I'll be lucky to get enough cars to ship more than two hundred at a time. So bring in two hundred and five and no culls."

"You'll break me," Kane said. "But after we get Ralston's shipped, I'll take the big ones at forty-two a head. I'll let you know how the rest goes. Getting enough cars is a problem."

Ben shook both men's hands. Mark and Chip did the same with polite nods.

"Kane. We weren't lucky. These boys are good," Ben said.

The cattle buyer looked hard at them and nodded sharply. "I guess so." Then he clucked to his team and wheeled them around.

"Tell us something, Ben," Chip said. "How'd you know they'd pay that?"

Ben watched a red-tailed hawk swoop across the herd. "I was holding the best hand in the poker game. If we'd come up here with mixed cattle or poor ones, we'd have been betting on the draw. We had four aces in these cattle. Those Mexicans never thought for one second that they wouldn't get them back to sell over again. Or we'd never have bought them like we did."

"You mean they sold them that cheap, not worrying they wouldn't get them back to sell again?" Mark dropped his gaze to the ground and shook his head.

"That's it, pard," Chip said, and bolted in the saddle. "You think Mark and I know enough to bring a herd up here?"

"Maybe," Ben said, and swung into the saddle.

"We got another test?" Chip asked.

"You go ride into Abilene and throw a damn two-day drunk, blow all your money, I'd say you'll never amount to more than hired help."

"That ain't no damn problem for me," Mark said.

Chip laughed. "Don't take no math expert to figure that trail bosses make more money than trail hands. Hell, rangers don't make any money. I won't worry about Abilene."

"How do we get the money to do this?" Mark asked as they rode back for camp.

"You two can have the difference between what I sell and the ones leftover, for starters." Ben held up his finger. "Providing you make it on my terms."

"Who'll buy them?" Mark asked.

"Some local butcher, or a farmer needing to raise some meat. You can go look for a buyer tomorrow."

"Can we both go look for a buyer tomorrow?"

"I reckon I can spare you two that long. But Thursday we need to be up and sorting come daylight."

"Them small steers won't be easy to get out either," Chip said, and they short-loped their horses for camp.

Ben bent over to refill his coffee cup from the pot in the twilight. Whippoorwills were all over the place, sounding off, and he nodded to Hap.

"Guess that means we'll head home soon?" Hap asked.

"I've been thinking all day." Ben glanced around to be certain no one was close enough to hear. "I'll need another buck-board in Texas."

"Ben McColloughie! I can ride a horse home."

"Yeah, and listen to you complain about that right hip clear past the Brazos?" He straightened and blew on his coffee. "Sell them mules and wagon. Buy me a buck-board and a good horse team."

"Where?"

"Abilene, I'd say. And we can sell thirty horses. Have Lou help you cut them out."

"Why . . . why . . . what if I don't get enough for them?"

"Hell, I don't care; what's left is your money."

"My . . . my money? You lost your mind. You owe the bank, the store, the hands' pay —"

"I sold twenty-eight thousand dollars' worth of cattle today. You take the money from the horses, mules, and wagon and buy me a buckboard and team out of it."

Hap closed his eyes. "You going back to buy another herd?"

Ben shook his head. "I'm going home to ranch. Buy some Durham bulls to cross on them longhorn cows. Buy some more land. A married man has no business trailing cattle this far from home."

"But . . . but —"

"No buts."

"I need a swallow of whiskey." Hap got up and, swinging his stiff leg, headed for the front of the wagon. He held the bottle up toward the firelight to measure the contents and nodded. "Two good snorts left."

With a head shake, Ben laughed aloud. "It ain't the end, old man."

"Ben McCollough settling down is sure the end." He took the rest of the liquor, then capped it with a deep "Ah."

"There's a job for you anytime, pard."

"Well, I wasn't planning on quitting," Hap said, and tossed the bottle away.

"Good, you ain't getting sentimental on me then."

"Ben McColloughie! I'll have you know . . ."

Not listening to Hap's ranting and rambling, Ben went and found his bedroll. It would be hard for him to sleep counting that much money. He looked at the starry sky. *Jenny, I'm coming home — rich, too. I'll buy you fancy things, darling.*

Chapter 24

A soft drizzle moistened his beard. Ben rode his stout bay horse called Blitz to the side of the steers. Stiffer-gaited than his other horses, the animal could catch anything, and Ben's concern that some of the steers might get a notion to break back for the herd had made him choose the bay.

"I counted 'em three times," Billy Jim said, "and so did Mark."

"Who's got the most schooling, you or him?" Ben asked.

"Lord, Ben, I don't know. We went about the same time to Mrs. Bryant's classes."

Ben laughed. "Didn't mean to upset you. I just wondered." He booted Blitz after a steer that broke from the procession and soon had him back.

"I ain't upset," Billy Jim said. "Fact, I'm sure glad you brought me along. I ain't been throwed since we got over the Arkansas. But I still put my catch rope on them. Just in case one gets real rowdy." He indicated the rope looped under his belt that went to the horse's head.

"Good idea. What you going to do when we get back?" Ben asked, watching another veil of rain sweep over the horizon.

"Can't say. You ain't going to make another drive, are you?"

"Don't plan to."

Bill nodded like he understood. "Then I'll look for work with someone else. I'm going to catch some cattle, too, this winter. Start me a herd of my own."

"Good luck," Ben said.

"Lord knows I'll need it. Got to get better at roping too."

"It'll come; you're a sticker."

Billy Jim beamed from his praise and went after the next steer starting to break away.

Cattle in the pens and counted, Ralston came over and gave Ben a receipt. "Pay you in the morning. They all look good. Wish more folks could bring in uniform cattle like these."

"They have to have a Mexican buyer," Ben said, and shared a private grin with Mark and Chip. "Let's get some lunch, boys, and head back. We've got lots of cutting to do."

"McCollough?" Kane came from the scale house, calling to him. "I'll be ready to start day after you finish with Ralston."

Ben gave him a salute off the brim of his hat. If things kept moving along he'd be home with his Jenny in no time. He and his four hands went across the tracks to the Lucky Tiger Saloon. "Order a beer and we can have the free lunch," he explained. "I'll pay for the beer."

He started to enter the bat-wing doors and a drunk in a suit staggered out. The haggard-looking, unshaven man raised his face, blinked his red eyes, and swore. "You sumbitch, you killed my brother!" He fumbled for a gun.

Ben's hand went for his Colt. Radamacher! Then Chip stepped in and cold cocked the man over the head with his pistol butt. He crumpled into a pile.

"Give me a hand, Mark," Chip said, bending over to pick him up by the arms. "Got to get this trash off the sidewalk."

"He was the one with them rustlers that night, wasn't he?" Billy Jim asked Ben under his breath.

"Yeah." Ben scowled after him as the boys dragged him by his arms around to the side and left him on the ground. Lucky for Radamacher that Chip had stepped in or he'd be pushing up daisies instead of sleeping off his drunk in the mud.

"Learned that in the rangers," Chip said.

"Disable them. Saves shooting them sometimes."

"Or puts it off for another time," Ben said softly, going inside. "But thanks anyway."

After they finished their lunch, they went back out. It was still cloudy, but the rain had lifted. They walked across the muddy street toward the pens and their saddle horses.

"No sign of him," Mark said, searching around.

"Radamacher ain't left the country; you can count on that," Ben promised him. He'd have to be wary of the phony buyer until they rode out for Texas.

Ralston paid Ben in gold for the steers at the scale office. "You aren't worried someone will rob you?" he asked, looking at the canvas sacks of double eagles on the counter.

"I won't need it if they do," Ben said.

"Why's that?"

" 'Cause it'll be over my dead body."

Ralston nodded as if considering the matter. "You're right."

With a nod, Ben packed a sack of coins in each side of his saddlebags, then the last two in Mark's. Mark hoisted his pouches to his shoulder and they headed for the door.

The Kane deal started in the next

morning. More rain threatened, and the big steers acted spooky at being separated. Ben held his breath until the first half was in the yards; then he rode back to relieve Hap, who was working on a mule sale.

"What're they worth?" Ben asked before Hap rode out, driving the team and mules. All the cooking gear and chuck boxes were piled on the ground with the bedrolls. Hap's canvas stretched over them on ropes strung from the cottonwoods and a few posts they'd cut for supports.

"I think six hundred."

"Whew," Ben said.

"You want out of the deal?" Hap asked sharply, ready to climb up.

"No, but you better get Lou to ride along with a spare hoss. You'll need a ride back."

"Yeah, that ain't a bad idea."

With a long exhale, Ben went to sit on the chuck box with enough gold inside it to buy a big place in Texas. Cash talked in the still war-battered economy at home. Even out on the frontier in Kansas things were better off than down there. He listened to thunder roll across the prairie. The storm was west of them and moving away. *Jenny, Jenny, I'm coming home.*

The buckboard with a well-broken team of sorrels cost Hap two hundred and fifty.

Hap had the man at the funeral home make him a box for the back with a false bottom to hide Ben's money. Then Hap bought a roll of canvas. The boys' ground cloths were worn out, so Hap and the boys cut out new ones for themselves and a cover for the box in the buckboard, which could be tied down with ropes.

Mark and Chip kept back six spare horses to pack or ride if another went lame after the boys each chose a favorite to ride back.

Hap sold the rest of the horses for fifteen apiece to the local liveryman. From the boys' sale of the culls, they deposited five hundred twenty-six dollars in Ben's make-shift bank. Hap's six hundred was there too.

Ben paid each hand the hundred dollars he owed them for the drive. "You ride back with us, I'll feed you and pay you another twenty five."

"When do we go back?" Toledo asked.

"How about day after tomorrow?" Ben asked them.

The crew's heads bobbed in agreement.

"Now you all can take your turn at the bright lights." Ben's words drew laughter from the crew. "But I need at least three men here in camp at all times. I'm going in and get the pack saddle and panniers I bought for the four packhorses."

"I help you," Lou said, and rushed off to get the four horses.

The gray buttermilk sky made a low ceiling like the belly of a gray goose, Ben decided, with the Asian riding beside him.

"What're you going to do next?" Ben asked his horse wrangler.

"Go home with you."

"I mean after this is over?"

"Could go work with uncle in laundry. Me like to be someone cookie. I watch Hap all the way. I cook too. What they pay cookie?"

"They pay two hundred to two-fifty."

"That good, me find outfit and be cookie."

"You need any recommendation, you tell them Ben McCollough said so."

"Me do that. More fun than laundry."

Ben dismounted at the livery stable. The rain had begun again. He was taking down his slicker when he heard the shout, and then he saw someone taking a shot at them, the blue smoke of a pistol in the person's hand. The shooter was coming down the street toward them.

"Ben! That crazy man shooting at us!" Lou screamed.

"I see him. Get some cover," Ben shouted at him, jerking the Spencer out of the scabbard. Radamacher had better have his funeral paid for.

"McCollough, you bastard!"

Folks were running for cover. Radamacher ranted aloud like a wild man. He fired another wild round that smacked into the livery's wooden front. Ben had him in his sights, curtained by the drizzle.

The Spencer slammed into Ben's shoulder when he squeezed the trigger. The .50-caliber lead bullet struck the cow buyer in the chest and propelled him backward. The Colt in his hand fired harmlessly into the air. A wild-eyed horse broke loose from the hitching rack in front of the Lucky Tiger and went bucking off in the light rain.

A fresh shell levered in the chamber, Ben waited. Radamacher lay sprawled on his back. His boots twisted in what Ben figured was his death throes. The drip of rain ran off his hat brim as he waited.

A man walked out and bent over Radamacher. "He's gone."

Ben nodded that he heard him and jammed the rifle into the scabbard. He gave a head toss to the cowering Lou that it was safe and started for the store across the street.

"Ain't you going to do anything about him?" the man called out.

"I already have," Ben said, and never looked back. Good riddance to bad company. Radamacher came looking for what he got.

That night in camp, everyone listened as the Asian told his version of the shoot-out. "Bullets, they go *zing-zing* all around. Lou, me get down. Think maybe he shoot me. Splinter wood on livery building. Ben, him no care, him get rifle-bang. Him shoot that crazy man. Man come 'cross street, him say him dead. Him ask Ben what you do about him? Ben say I do it already."

The boys all laughed.

"If you all have your business done, we'll head for home in the morning." Ben looked over their deeply tanned faces in the firelight.

"Man, you were right about the ugly women," Billy Jim said, sitting on the ground, pulling off his new boots. "They were double ugly."

"I told you go to Mexico with me," Miguel said, and shook his head.

"Well, I never spent no money here on any," Billy Jim said, "that's for damn sure."

Everyone laughed.

The days grew warmer and longer. They

pushed hard for home and in a week rode past Dru's cross. They used the logs left on the bank to float the buckboard, which made the Arkansas ford uneventful. Days grew longer and Ben pushed for thirty miles a day, doubling the miles a day they had driven the cattle. They avoided Indian settlements. He had Mark and Chip taking turns each day scouting their route.

They talked to other drovers heading north with herds in a steady stream. Was McCoy's situation like he said, or a joke? How was this and that crossing? Had they seen so-and-so along the way?

They stopped over in San Antonio for hot baths in a tub, shaves for those needing one, and haircuts. In the Cattleman's Hotel, with their money locked in the safe, they soon were beseeched with inquiries about the drive.

"Sam Gaines from Delo County," a man in a white business suit introduced himself as the crew sat around eating supper, less Digger and Lou, who had gone off on their own. "I understand you boys just got back from Kansas."

"That's right, sir," Mark said.

"You the man?" Gaines asked Ben rather pointedly.

Ben shook his head. "Mark and Chip here

can tell you all you want to know, sir."

"But they're only boys. I need a man —"

"Mister." Ben looked up, his patience short. "If you need some drovers, they can do it."

"Oh."

"Mr. Gaines, was it?" Chip stood up astraddle his chair and offered his hand. "What kind of cattle do you have?"

"What do you mean what kind? I've got longhorns."

"Well, sir, it will make a big difference when you get there. . . ."

Mark, also standing, agreed. Those two boys would make it. Ben forked in another bite of the grilled beef. Things simply tasted better cooked over mesquite.

After the big meal, the two boys were off talking with their next employer.

"I bet those two want to go look at his herd," Ben said to the Mexican boys and Hap.

"You know, I been thinking," Hap said. "I may sign on with them boys. They'll sure need a cook."

"They'll sure need one," Ben said. "I ain't running you off, am I?"

"Lord, no."

"Hap, you and the boys deliver that money to the bank. I want to ride ahead. I can be there in two days' hard riding," Ben said.

"You leaving right now?" Hap asked.

"Yeah."

"You could wait till daylight."

Ben clapped him on the shoulder. He'd damn sure miss Hap. "I've already paid Digger and Lou. Pay the rest the twenty-five I owe them when you get to Teeville."

"I'll stick the rest in the bank," Hap said.

"Good. What do I owe you?" Ben looked hard at the man he'd spent over five years with.

"I'll be at your wedding. Give you a bill then."

"Just so you got one when you get there." Ben nodded to the others. "Thanks, see you all at home."

He felt anxious as he headed for the livery on the far side of the square. The old Alamo church belfry stood out against the starry sky as he took large strides. *Jenny, I'm coming.*

Chapter 25

Ben felt the heat of the morning rising from the ground as he short-loped Roan. It was less than two miles to Jenny's. Anticipation coursed through his veins. So close, so near to her. The drum of Roan's hooves on the ground made a song. He could hardly wait to hold and squeeze her, tell her all the news of the drive, and just be in her company.

He rode into the yard and blinked. Something was wrong. The place looked deserted. He bolted off of Roan and ran for the porch. When his hand touched the door, it swung open and he stared inside.

There was no smell of her cooking or perfume when he stepped inside. He even saw traces of cobwebs on things; no one had been here in some time. Were she and the boys at his place? He rushed outside, consumed with fear, swung aboard Roan, and rushed for the MC.

He crossed the creek, pushing the hard-breathing Roan, and saw no activity around the home place, no horses in the corrals. Where was she? He dropped from the saddle; the hard ride over the past forty-eight hours had sapped him. Not finding her only added to his confusion.

He ducked the lintel and pushed the door in. No one had been there either recently. What in the devil was going on? Perhaps if he caught another ranch horse . . . Roan was tired, done in. Maybe Deputy Kilmer could tell him where she was at, though dread knotted his stomach over his suspicion of the truth.

He rode the roan down in the meadow and roped a fresh pony — the dun mare that Billy Jim had used to break the mules. He saddled her and left Roan to rest. In a long lope he headed for Teeville. *Jenny, I'm coming. Lord, make her be all right.*

It was past sunset when he rode up to Kilmer's small frame house on the edge of town. He dismounted after checking around and headed up the path to the front door.

"That you, Ben?" the deputy asked, wiping his face on a napkin and getting up from his supper table.

"What's happened?" Ben asked, nodding to the man's wife.

"Ben, you better sit down. I've got some

hard news for you."

"Tell me."

"Jenny Fulton's dead. Her youngest, Ivory, is dead, and the middle boy, Tad, is over at Doc's. He may not live."

"What happened?"

"According to Tad, Coulter came by with several of his kin. Jenny threatened them with a shotgun. Someone shot her. Tad said it was Harold did the shooting. Coulter said if he couldn't have her, no one would. Then the bunch shot the boys so they couldn't talk. Tad's alive, but . . . well, he might not make it. Been touch-and-go for months."

"Did you arrest them?"

"Only evidence I got is that boy's say-so against six or seven of them." Kilmer shook his head. "Don't go get it in your head to revenge this. Let the law work."

"Work? When did they bury her?"

"About the fifteenth of May."

"Why didn't you wire me?"

"How in the devil was I supposed to know where you were?"

"Coulter and his bunch still out on the loose?"

"Yeah, sorry as that sounds, they are."

"What's the sheriff say?"

"We ain't got much of a case. Where you going?"

"To make a case." Ben hurried outside and ignored Kilmer's warning. He bounded into the saddle and headed for Doc's. He wanted a list of their names from Tad.

Doc's office was above the saddle shop. He left the dun in the alley so no one recognized her and made the stairs two at a time. Through the glass pane in the door he saw no one was inside and twisted the knob. Once in the office he headed for the room where Doc kept patients.

Slowly he opened the knob and pushed in the door. Light from the office flooded in onto the bed, and Ben looked shocked at the snowy, drawn face of the boy.

"Ben?" he asked in a cracked voice. "Ben, that you?"

"Yes," he said, and knelt beside the bed.

"Ben, I tried to stop them. Tell Mark I really tried. I got one with a pitchfork — but they shot Ivory in the head, Ben."

"Who was there that day, Tad?" Ben took out his tally book.

"John Coulter, Sam, his brother. Martin and Boyd —" Tad's coughing cut off his speech. "Them's the Billings brothers."

Ben nodded. He hoped this effort would not set the boy back. The way the coughing racked him, he wondered if his lungs had been riddled.

"Dude . . . Pickett, Curly Morgan." Tad shook his head on the pillow as if to try to clear it. "Rusty was there."

"Stevens?"

"Yeah, him. Ben, I've had lots of fever. But I seen them all there. Coulter shot Mom like she was a dog."

"Rest easy. Mark will soon be back to take care of you. He's on his way now."

"Oh, good. But will he blame me for what happened?"

"No, Tad, he won't blame you. Nothing you could have done about it. Rest now. I'll be back and we'll talk some more."

"Ben? I'm sure glad you're here. I worried you'd never come back." Tears began to roll down the boy's pale cheeks.

"I'm back, and we'll settle this."

"I know you will. They buried her and Ivory up by the Stallings Schoolhouse."

"Thanks," Ben said, and left the room, closing the door behind him. Doc must be off making rounds. He'd need to locate the killers next. Heading out of the office, he jammed the tally book in his vest pocket.

He rode the dun out to the schoolhouse and found the two mounds in the starlight, settled down by the rain and the months since their interment. He struck a match and read her name on the faded board cross. *Jenny Fulton.*

A knot crawled up his throat and threatened to choke him. His vision grew blurry and all he could manage to shout was, "Why, Jenny?"

Sunup came peeking through the cedars and struck on the low-roofed cabin of squared logs. A man in his underwear with a smoker's cough came out barefooted and started to relieve his bladder ten feet from the front door.

"Curly Morgan?" Ben asked, sitting on the bench with his back to the wall.

"Who —"

"You were there the day they shot her and the boys, weren't you?"

"Huh?" The man whirled and his eyes flew wide open. "I never —"

"Never what? Shot her? Harold did that. You shot that little boy in the back of the head, didn't you?"

"No!" His voice quavered. "That was Rusty. I swear to Gawd, I never wanted to be there. I told them to stop. I said we'd all be in trouble; they never listened."

"You been keeping bad company, Morgan. Them Coulters your cousins?"

"Yeah, but I never knowed what they aimed to do when they rode by that place.

Harold said she was sweet on him. McCollough, I swear to Gawd I never knew nothing he planned to do that day."

"Just sort of happened when she got out the shotgun, huh?"

"No! I couldn't believe he shot her. Harold went crazy — I mean lost his mind. Then his brother Sam said, 'We got to get them boys; they's witnesses.' "

"Who got the pitchforking?"

"Martin Billings. Course, they couldn't take him to the doc here. Took him clear to Mason. Some old German doctor worked on him up there — he ain't done no good either."

"I'll tell the boy he did do some good, huh?"

Curly batted his eyes at Ben. "He still alive?"

A black cloud flew over Ben's mind. "Why, was Harold going to kill him too?"

"Thought he —"

"Gawdamn you!" Ben cursed and gritted his teeth, and the Navy Colt spoke in his hands. He knew what the man intended to say — Coulter was supposed to have eliminated Tad already. Curly threw his arms up and flopped over on the ground with three .44 slugs in his chest. Through a haze of gunsmoke, Ben could see the red blood spill out onto the man's gray underwear.

They intended to silence the boy. They might have already done that. He'd better get back to Teeville. He could hope he wasn't too late. He gathered up his reins and rode hard for town.

Chapter 26

At midday, out of breath, Ben hurried up the stairs to the doc's office. Nothing looked out of place in the street. He took the stairs two at a time and burst in to see the shocked face of the physician and a lady sitting in a seat in front of him.

"The boy?" Ben gasped. "He all right?"

"Certainly, why?" Doc asked, standing up.

" 'Cause the Coulters are planning on killing him."

"He's no threat to them."

"Ma'am, I'm sorry you're a party to this, but a gang member, Curly Morgan, told me so."

The lady gasped and held her kerchief to her mouth.

"I'll go get Kilmer and have him guard the place. Mrs. Bowman, take these pills and maybe it will go away." Doc handed her a small bottle. "One in the morning, one at night. I better go get that deputy. Excuse me."

"Yes, Doctor," she said, and rose. She nodded to Ben and started for the door. The physician was putting on his coat. At the sounds of shouting, Ben reached over, caught her by the arm and pulled her back. The middle-aged woman gave a yelp.

"Stay here!" Ben said, and stuck his head out the door to look down the stairs, but he could not see what the ruckus in the street was about. Gun in hand, he started down the stairs. There were shots and then someone familiar reined his horse up at the bottom of the stairs.

Sam Coulter, seeing him, shouted, "Damn! McCollough's back."

Ben took aim and shot the man off his horse. Sam's last bullet struck the wood close by Ben's hand and splintered the siding. He lost no time bailing down the stairs. He had one shot left in his cap-and-ball; he regretted not reloading after he left Morgan's. Someone over by the store across the street drew his fire. *Missed — damn.*

Ben felt a hot knife crease his leg. He was hit. His own gun empty, Ben ran for the rear and the Spencer on the saddle. Two more wild shots whizzed over his head. He jerked the Spencer out and managed to grab two tubes of ammo from his saddlebags.

"Ben, this way," a voice hissed.

Millescent, with an impatient look on her face, waved at him from the back door of the saloon, the one husbands exited after a trip to see some dove. The blood was warm oozing down his leg into his boot. It felt on fire, but he could stand the pain up to a point. A quick check and he ducked inside.

"How many are there?" he asked.

She shook her head. "Five or six. They've shot you. Got Kilmer and Doc out front. Oh, no, you're bleeding."

"I need to get upstairs, where I can watch Doc's stairs and make sure they can't get up there to the boy next door."

"The corner room?" she asked, gathering up the volumes of material in the duster she wore and running down the hallway.

"You have any guns in here, and ammo?"

"There's two shotguns down in the bar. I'll get them."

He nodded, and she used a key to open the door for him.

"I'm worried about your leg."

"Get the guns," he said. "We can worry about that later."

A young woman awakened by their entrance screamed, but Millescent waved her from the bed and told her to shut up. "I'll get those guns, Ben."

He rushed to the side window and saw

Dude Pickett, gun in hand, halfway up the stairs.

"Pickett!" Ben shouted as he took sight, squeezed the trigger, and the rifle stock slammed into his shoulder. Struck hard by the .50-caliber bullet, Pickett did a cartwheel downward, and someone took a potshot at Ben that splintered the side of the window casing. He drew back and levered another shell into the rifle chamber. At the front window, he took a shot and knocked down the mousy-colored horse Boyd Billings rode. Billings dove for the ground and scrambled like a wildcat for the porch of the millinery.

Aside from scattered cussing, there were no sounds. The street was empty. Millescent was tearing up a sheet for bandages. A pistol-shaped sawed-off doublebarrel was on the bed; so was a long-stocked one, several brass shells laid beside them. They'd do for a standoff at close range.

"Let me check your leg," she said.

He stood back aside from the window, where he could view part of the street and be out of a bullet's pathway.

"When did you go to worrying about me?" he demanded.

"Well, I had to choose sides, and I figured you needed help worse than they did." She shook her head so her hair bounced. "I ain't so damn sure now. How many are left?"

"Three of 'em, I figure. Unless they got more help."

She brought a chair over and forced him to sit down. "You're a bloody mess, you know that?"

"Too far from my heart to kill me."

"Damn it, sit still. I'm going to cut your pants away from it." He glanced down and frowned at the pigsticker she was using to slice away the material.

"Be careful where you put that thing."

She was kneeling on the floor and looked up to give him a scowl. "Sit down and get your finger off the trigger. I'm going to use whiskey to clean it."

"Here," he said, taking the bottle from her. "I need some of that." A quick swallow ran like fire down his throat and all the way to his empty stomach. The leg hurt worse than he wanted to think about — he sucked in his breath when she put the whiskey to it.

"You always have been hardheaded —" Her words were broken off by bullets shattering the top glass out of the street-side window that was open for ventilation.

"Got to be certain they can't get up those stairs to Doc's. They're wanting to kill Tad Fulton so he can't testify."

She nodded and wrapped the bandages tight around his exposed leg. Then she tied them off with a hard pull.

"That should stop some of the bleeding. I think everyone has fled this building. I'll try to make sure no one comes up the stairs."

"Good." He looked at the blood all over her once-fresh duster.

"I know, I'm bloody, but that will wash away. So don't you bleed to death before this is over." She stood up, holding her hands out, and headed for the pitcher and bowl on the stand.

He turned his attention to the street out front. Where was Kilmer? She'd said they had shot the deputy. No telling. He caught sight of a hat at the edge of the millinery porch roof and took aim. Three shots answered him, but by then he was back enough that they either plowed into the wood siding or the tin tile ceiling above him.

When he looked again she was on the bed dressed only in a corset. Obviously she'd shed the cumbersome duster. With care she was loading the double-barrel.

"There's only three left out there by my count," he said, crossing to look out the side window at Doc's staircase.

"Who's that again?" she asked, tugging

up the corset with both hands to hold herself in it.

"John Coulter, Rusty Stevens, and Boyd Billings. Morgan said that Martin Billings might die from the pitchfork wounds Tad gave him."

"I hadn't seen him in days. That's why, I guess," she said, standing to the side of the front window and watching the street.

"They're under the millinery porch."

She nodded and used her hands to push her hair back. He took a good look at her before he turned back to watch the stairs. Less than five feet tall, wearing a snow-white corset that only defined her figure, she still took his breath — even at times like this. *Damn.* Nothing was down there but the lengthening shadows of afternoon.

"Where is everyone?" she demanded with her bare shoulders pressed to the plaster wall. "Someone surely knows by now what those bastards are doing. Isn't there anyone in this town with guts enough to help you?"

"You," he said, and turned back to check on the stairs.

"All right, I'm a fool."

Ben turned and frowned at her words — she looked crestfallen, with her chin down.

"I'm the damn fool," she said.

"For being here now? You can still get

out." Where were they? Why didn't they stick their head out?

"That's not what I'm talking about!"

"Good, spill it. This leg is biting me. Three guys down there on the street want me and a boy dead."

"Aw, hell, you wouldn't care anyway even if you didn't have all this to bother you."

He strode across, acting as though the fire in his leg weren't anything, but his blood was already saturating the bandage. Either way he looked outside there was nothing in sight.

Were they waiting for dark? No telling, but until they had him and the boy silenced, they wouldn't give up.

"McCollough!" It was John Coulter's voice.

"Go ahead!"

"You might just as well give up. Throw down your gun and come out or we're gonna kill you."

"They will anyway," Milly said in a stage whisper that carried enough fire, Ben decided, that her words must have scorched the window facing's paint.

"They'll pry my dead fingers off this gun's trigger first," he said to her.

She nodded sharply. "Damn right."

"Won't do no good to keep shooting; you

ain't getting us," Coulter shouted back.

"I haven't done so bad so far," he said to her.

She nodded with a smug set to her full lips. "It's his bravado talking. Probably drinking. He'll get drunk enough to think he's invincible in a little while."

Ben nodded. That would be what he needed. Boyd Billings was a kid. Not very tough, by Ben's standards. Rusty was the real danger, besides John himself. So he had two tough adversaries out there.

A barrage of shots rang out. Ben jerked Milly away from the window and wall, his boot soles crunching the broken glass as he spun her behind him. For a brief second he turned to look over his shoulder and met her pale blue gaze. The reality of the bullets crashing into the building made him back up farther in the cloud of plaster dust until they both fell on the bed.

The slick dust billowed in the air, and they hear the ear-shattering crash of lead into the structure, up to the ceiling tiles and ricocheting like mad hornets across them. On their backs, side by side, Ben looked over at Milly and shook his head in disapproval over the shooting. Clenched-teeth anger made sharp bolts of chill run up his face.

"Well, we're back in bed again," she said, and laughed as they lay on their backs waiting for the shooting to stop.

"It's a diversion," Ben said, and jumped up. He grabbed the shotgun and at the side window saw Boyd Billings, pistol in hand, halfway up the staircase. He took aim on the wide-eyed twenty-year-old's chest. The scattergun roared so loud it hurt Ben's ears. The black powder smoke cleared in seconds. Ben watched Billings tumble down the steps and lie in death's arms at the bottom. A scarlet wound the size of a bucket covered his chest.

"Gawdamn you, McCollough," John screamed.

"Give me the rifle," Ben said. His leg handicapping his gait, he tossed Milly the shotgun as he hobbled to the front window, hoping for a shot at the outraged Coulter. She brought him the Spencer.

"What now?" she asked.

"Riders are coming," he said, the gun's ringing still in his ears.

"Who could that be?"

"Might be my crew. I don't want them to ride into a trap."

"How we going to warn them?" she asked, frowning, her thin brows drawn.

"Go to shooting like hell when they get

close to put them on guard. Get me those tubes off the bed."

"Sure."

Ben crossed to the other side of the window. He could see the riders' dust. They were about to enter the town perhaps a block away. He switched sides and started shooting into the street, raising a cloud of dirt that would upset anyone, he figured. Then he loaded another tube into the rifle's butt and worked the lever rapid-fire.

"You think you warned them?" she asked. Her hand was on his shoulder as they waited in the cloud of black powder smoke. They heard no sounds of horses.

"What the hell's going on?" Chip called out.

"Coulter's got me treed!" Ben shouted back.

"They down here?"

"They were."

"You all right, Ben?" Mark yelled at him from the street.

"Fine, go up into Doc's office. See how Tad is."

"Tad?"

"Your brother," Millescent yelled. "And you others get up here; this big galoot is about to pass out on me. He's been shot."

Chapter 27

Ben had the crutch under his right arm to keep weight off his leg. He was looking at Mark and Chip sitting their horses.

"You boys remember, those rivers deserve respecting. Treat his cattle like they were your own. Don't take the first offer either."

"We won't," Mark said. "We think we can get up there before the weather turns bad this fall," Mark said. "Hap and the boys are going to be mad waiting on us up there."

"Knowing Hap, he might start out without you," Ben said, and nodded at Milly, who came out to join him, drying her hands.

"Tad's coming here next week," she said. "Doc says he's recovering fine. Tad can help old crip here and they both can get well together."

"Thanks, ma'am," Chip said, and touched his hat.

"Ben, we'll be thinking about you," Mark said. "And make Tad mind."

"I will. You boys better ride. Daylight's burning," Ben said.

He stood with Milly beside him and watched the two gallop away. It was risky business going north this late in the year, but the man who owned the cattle wanted the boys to try to get them up there and sold. They'd learn a lot. A hell of a lot.

"Well, I'm glad they have Coulter and the other two in jail," she said. "One less thing for you to worry about."

"Me worry?" Ben laughed, and started back into the house after her.

When she reached the wood cook range, she turned and put her hands on her hips. Wearing a proper dress for a rancher's wife, blue with ruffles down the front, she looked half civilized, Ben decided.

"Ben McCollough, you still set on us getting married?"

"Millescent, I'm dead serious."

She ran over and hugged him. "I am, too."

Epilogue

Amid the tall untrimmed grass stems and dry weed stalks, Ben and Millescent McCollough's graves are side by side at the Stallings Schoolhouse cemetery. His marble marker says, *Capt. Benjamin McCollough, Army CFSA, "Best man ever went up the Abilene Trail." Died June 10, 1898.* Beside him is her marker, which reads, *Millescent Jane McCollough, "The woman who tamed him."* She preceded him in death by five years.

Tad Fulton, their stepson and the only heir to the eight-thousand-acre ranch, used the MC brand until his death in 1936. His son, Benjamin, passed it on to his boy, Benjamin the third, who still uses the MC hot iron on his cattle to this day in Kerr Mac County, Texas.

About the Author

Ralph Compton stood six-foot-eight without his boots. He worked as a musician, a radio announcer, a songwriter, and a newspaper columnist. His first novel, *The Goodnight Trail*, was a finalist for the Western Writers of America's Medicine Pipe Bearer Award for best debut novel. He is also the author of the *Sundown Riders* series and the *Border Empire* series.

The employees of Thorndike Press hope you have enjoyed this Large Print book. All our Thorndike and Wheeler Large Print titles are designed for easy reading, and all our books are made to last. Other Thorndike Press Large Print books are available at your library, through selected bookstores, or directly from us.

For information about titles, please call:

(800) 223-1244

or visit our Web site at:

www.gale.com/thorndike
www.gale.com/wheeler

To share your comments, please write:

Publisher
Thorndike Press
295 Kennedy Memorial Drive
Waterville, ME   04901